GERRY'S SUMMER

by

Ian MacTavish

First published by KDP in the USA in 2021

Copyright © Ian MacTavish 2021

The moral right of the author has been asserted.

Author: Ian MacTavish 1940 –
Title: Gerry's Summer/Ian MacTavish
ISBN: 978-0-6451377-1-2

Fiction.

Cover design: Fran Allan.
11 pt Cambria

Chapter One

In the growing heat of the first full day of summer, Mum sat on a bench in Hyde Park reading again her sister's words. She wondered again which version was true.

Before she died her sister had once insisted it really happened to her.

But had also said she thought it was a great idea to start a novel.

Mum had only a few things that belonged to her sister. Apart from some books with her name written on the flyleaf, this square was the only piece in her handwriting. Her sister had talked about becoming a writer but Mum had never seen a typed word.

She looked at the unfolded page again.

"Years ago I was on a bus to visit my mother's grave. In the seat in front was a girl seven or eight, about the age I had been when my mother died. I noticed the girl wore a gold bracelet with an engraved heart. As the bus lurched the girl reached forward to grab a rail and I could read entwined the initials PSM. The same as mine, I thought.

I got off at the stop before the gate and went to buy

some flowers. By the time I walked through the trees to the grave, I saw the girl from the bus just standing up from kneeling at my mother's headstone. I paused and before I could call out, the girl walked away down another path clearly wiping her eyes."

Mum thought back to when their mother had died. Mum had married and had moved interstate since then and didn't know about her sister's visits to their mother's grave. She tried to put a time frame on things, to bring forward clear pictures of her mother and her sister and remember the milestones as they grew up; the house, the pets, the holidays, their father, but her mind simply returned to what was on the page. True story? Then who was the girl?

The day was going to be a scorcher.

It was still just before noon and she could feel it already, even though she was under the shade of a huge Port Jackson fig tree, with the faintest mist of moisture coming from the spray of the Archibald Fountain to her left.

She could hear the traffic slightly muted and the high noise of some cicadas further down the Park.

Mum loved the summer almost as much as Dad and the kids, but a girl still had to stay cool. She had done some shopping in the city and had a large bottle of ginger beer in her bag. She wouldn't wait till she got home. I'm a big girl, she thought. I can do what I like ... even swig from the bottle in public.

It was still cold as she eased it out of her bag. The moisture on the surface slipped under her fingers and the bottle took off with a huge bounce.

Wow. You should've seen it go, she would say later.

It was like it had a rocket up its bum. I've never seen anything like it.

It rolled across the bare dirt surrounding the base of the tree as though it had a mind of its own. It leapt a root and rolled some more and landed up against a rock on the other side, moving the rock a few centimetres and wedging itself under the rough edge.

She looked around to see if anyone else had watched this insane behaviour.

That's all I need. Inanimate objects with magic powers, deciding when and where they'll jump. Next, they'll be taking over the world.

She stood up to fetch the defiant container, its contents now whitened with froth.

Moving the rock as she retrieved the bottle she saw a small hole in the ground. She could just make out the dusty brown nose of an emerging cicada. She watched for a minute and it came forward moving very slowly in its shell, shedding bits of dirt as it headed for the main trunk of the tree. She reached down to pick it up carefully with a thumb and forefinger, taking a couple of steps across the roots and holding it steady until it attached itself in a vertical fold in the grey bark which she hoped would offer some concealment.

"There you go, young man. That'll save you a walk. You're probably very tired. I don't know how long you've been banging your head on that rock."

The cicada climbed with a straight faced determination. Mum hadn't time to wait and observe the whole cycle of emergence.

"Well, you are a very lucky little chap. This is your first day and it's a good one too."

Chapter Two

The next morning, with another warm day in the making, Tim was working on his best ever toast.

He was usually the first up. In his early life he had been the cause of much tiredness in the family, but these days he was a regular and welcoming alarm clock, always full of the joys of life.

Mum was usually next, then Dad, then always last, Ellie. The serious sleepyhead.

Mum was sitting watching Tim's performance with a vague sense of unease. Nothing to do with toast. What was it?

She went to her bag and pulled out the square of paper. She didn't open it but held it in her hands feeling the folds as though they were a favourite fabric. She waited for Dad.

She was about to witness a very small event in the history of the world, but one in a trail of small happenings, in which some modest people began to address some fundamental imbalances of life.

Tim's toast, responding to a final sweep of the knife, slipped off the plate to the bench and onto the floor.

He'd made two lovely pieces, with too much butter and plenty of Vegemite. He'd spread them one after the other very carefully to the edge of the crusts, not missing a millimetre.

He held the knife in his fist as children do, but he had a very delicate and accurate touch.

His secret was holding the tip of his tongue in the corner of his lips.

The natural goodness and tenacity of the Vegemite stifled any possible bounce.

The toast lay there, its bare backside staring at Tim's open mouth.

He was still young enough to cry at misfortune, but Tim wasn't given to softness on any of his projects. He was a great maker of things, and had already learned that crying gets you nowhere.

It cuts no ice with most of the bits of stuff you have to work with in this world.

Inanimate objects have hearts of stone. Even if they could hear you they'd take no notice.

Dad walked past buttoning his shirt. He looked at the problem.

Tim looked up, anticipating wisdom.

"Toast *always* falls buttered side down. It has ever since bread was invented. There are carvings in the Great Pyramid showing Pharaohs looking down at their toast with tears in their eyes. My grandfather told me that."

Mum stepped up to touch Tim's helmet of white hair. She crouched down and picked up the toast, dropped it in the bin and reached for the paper towel.

"Don't worry, sweetheart. Mum will make you another one."

"I'd rather do it myself. I had that one just right."

"OK. Go for it."

Dad believed in the five second rule. He would have picked it up and eaten it if it were his.

Tim returned to the toaster with a fresh slice of bread. He hovered, looking down at the floor where Mum had wiped. He wondered if untoasted bread behaved the same way when it was buttered. Did the toasting process have something to do with it?

His father saw him wondering. They were very close. Both very practical men, good with their hands. They both pondered mechanical things in a way a woman never would. Or most men for that matter.

"Raw bread does exactly the same thing. You don't

have to test it. Your father told you that."

Tim knew he was right.

Dad, who had just picked his toothbrush out of the toilet bowl, was wondering why so many everyday objects were so ... what?

Uncooperative? Calculating? Ornery?

Falling toast should be a fifty/fifty option. But it's not.

A toothbrush slipping from the fingers directly above a bathroom basin should fall harmlessly into that basin. It should not catch the corner of the tap, somersault to the edge, spring with a power previously undetected in toothbrushes, over to the towel rail, slide down the wall tiles and with a final flick, absolutely dead centre on the thin pipe beside the cistern, spiral itself into the clear pool of the toilet.

It shouldn't do that.

Dad had scrubbed the toothbrush in soap and hot water and poured some Dettol over it while wondering at its Olympian performance. That's what really got to him, as it did every time something like this happened. You could not do that again if you tried. You could not do that in a million years. If someone offered you a million dollars to do it again you could stay there for the rest of your life taking sleep breaks once a day, with family and friends bringing you sustenance on the hour and still you could never do it again. Why, on this one simple drop, on this morning when he was in a hurry, would it do that to him!

Why does a toothbrush exhibit that level of bastardry only when it has a chance to cause such mischief? If you dropped it outside the bathroom it would just drop.

The event reminded him of the wayward screw on the weekend. The only one from the well-filled jar of assorted screws that would fit the work he was doing on the wooden decking. He dropped it and watched it leap sideways a full metre, disappearing down the only gap of all the gaps for two metres in either direction that was two millimetres wider than the rest. He knew because he just had to measure them all. If it had bounced to any other crack he could have retrieved it.

But no, it now meant a trip to the hardware shop to buy a pack of fifty the same size. He didn't need fifty. Just one.

You couldn't do that again in a million years. How did it know to go for that one gap!

Dad was still shaking his head over the screw as he

walked from the bathroom, having resolved not to tell the girls about the toothbrush. They would only go "Ooooh Daaaad!", put on the rubber gloves, grab his toothbrush and throw it in the bin. You can't buy a new utensil every time you think a germ may be lurking. There'd probably be more germs on the rubber gloves than there would be down that bowl. Dad often expressed the opinion that half the kids in Australia these days have asthma and allergies because they didn't meet enough germs when they were babies. More food off the floor, more dog hair, more dirt and snails from the garden would have done them all good.

"But Daaaad," Ellie had said the first time he told her, "Tim and I don't have asthma. Don't tell me you gave us snails."

"No darling. Your mum said you were too pretty and wouldn't let me give you snails."

"Thankyou."

"Tim got the snails. I gave you lizards."

"Aaaaagh!"

On this hot Sydney morning, in rapid succession, Dad had witnessed the Tantalising Toothbrush and the Tantrum Toast. Too close, he thought. Could they somehow be connected, and was the Sneaky Screw in on it? Are these events on the increase?

Mum squeezed past him as he was wondering.

"You would have picked that up, wouldn't you? If I wasn't here."

"Of course. It's a Rule. Germs have to stay behind the line and not move for five seconds and are therefore not present on anything that drops on the floor as long as you pick it up straight away."

"Rubbish." She punched him on the arm. "Another of your Grand Theories."

"Not a Theory. A Rule."

She held up the folded paper.

"Can you remember where I got this? Was there any more of it?"

Dad looked closely as she unfolded the lined page so he could read the writing.

"Your sister's. Ummm. You found it. Wasn't it in an envelope? Or a box. A shoebox. You found that in a purse in a shoebox. I remember you found the purse and took it out. I don't think you went through it all. There may be more in there."

"Where's the box, now?"

"Up the back in the trunk. Might be under the house."

Chapter Three

The heart of Sydney is not grand.

There are no fabulous squares, plazas or piazzas. No wide avenues or splendid vistas.

The streets are said to have followed the horse and cart tracks from the early days. Or even the original aboriginal foot-tracks along the sandstone ridges. Today, crammed with cars, they seem not much wider than that. The roads as originally laid out are constrained by the major and now immovable buildings; they were positioned by men who had no grand ambitions, no vision for a Great City of the South. They simply formalised what seemed to be adequate at the time.

There was no master plan for numbered avenues and streets like New York, or the boulevards and hubs of Paris with their clear lines of fire. Without a war or a conflagration to encourage a fresh start, this measly layout has stayed the same for a couple of centuries. For efficiency it can't even match the central grid squares of Melbourne or Adelaide. Sydney just sort of grew.

Today, half a dozen narrow streets make their way uptown from the water at Circular Quay and are crossed by an irregular hatching of even smaller side streets and lanes.

This unplanned development has however left some sweet legacies.

In a small street not far from the site of the original Government House, there is a row of terrace houses. Just four or five stories high, almost lost beneath the megatowers recently built to rise above and around them, they have survived since the late Victorian age and are now restored and preserved for all times. Hopefully. The space they occupy although absolutely prime in itself is now incorporated into the total development of the block. In the future will they always be considered too small to excite even the most rapacious developer?

People wonder why they are still here in this city which largely rubbled its history in the sixties and seventies to go relentlessly up with modern glass and concrete.

Could it be something to do with the ownership? Who did own them for so long? Maybe an old family was running a business there or living there and didn't want to sell when early developers were out with their chequebooks trying to consolidate the area. A more recent heritage listing could have something to do with it. Maybe all the money in the world wouldn't let you knock them down now.

Imagine owning a modest gem like that right in the middle of the city. What a good home it could make!

Dad was sketching the dream with a draughtsman's sure hand on the back of some papers from his brief case. He was seated at the bus stop opposite, in front of a lovely sandstone building where he often sat when he had finished his business in town. He'd take a pause in this quiet spot before walking home across Hyde Park. It was hot and humid this evening, but Dad never wore a jacket and tie so he felt better off than the men in suits, and some of the women, who paraded moistly past.

He was happy drawing once again some of his favourite buildings in the city. Ticking in the detail of the ironwork. Capturing the lines of the carved stone and the round topped windows. Does anyone make curved timber windows anymore?

If this house was ours the cellar would be my workshop and wine storage.

We'd put the kitchen, dining and family room on the first floor. Give the kids half a floor each. Mum and I would share a floor. Up top would be a guest floor with entertaining areas. Would there be a view back to the Harbour from the top? Not likely. Big buildings would block it for sure. The roof behind the peak of that facade is probably just timber and corrugated iron. We'd reinforce the roof and put in a pool. Of course we would. This is a fantasy. No room for a garage. Hey, we walk everywhere anyway. We'll hire a car if we need it on weekends.

He sat back to complete his sketch, checking the dimensions once again against the real thing, bottom to top.

He saw a tiny speck, too small for a bird, buzz around and then fly into a top floor window.

The tiny speck was Gerry Greengrocer, late for dinner again.

Clearing the windowsill he flew up to the round table where the cicadas dined every evening.

There were forty or so of them tonight, like Arthur's knights in a tiny circle.

Mostly they were Greengrocers, but there were some cousins as well, Yellow Mondays and a Chocolate

Soldier. They all nodded to Gerry and kept sipping.

Cicadas are unfailingly polite but never effusive. Gerry fluttered in between Garth and George, both much older than him. Four or five days at least.

He was quite excited and took a couple of seconds to shimmy his wings into their resting position. George and Garth didn't mind. They'd known excitement in their lives too.

"I met a cat today, and he seemed to be alright." He chirruped loudly.

"Nonsense, Young Gerry." Gwynneth called out imperiously from across the table. "We don't have anything to do with cats. For obvious reasons." Gwynneth was the most senior female and was crawling along the top of the small gum tree branch resting on her side of the table.

Each of the cicadas had a similar green branch with several twigs and a fan of leaves in front of them.

There was a pile of extra branches that had been laid in the middle of the table for any uncounted visitors or if anyone felt like sucking more than they had in front of them. The pile held a selection of eucalyptus sprigs. There were some camphorlaurel for variety and a few slips of casurina which the Tom

Thumbs usually liked.

"But this one was quite friendly," Gerry continued. "He walked right up behind me without pouncing, I didn't even hear his footsteps. It was only when he made a sort of 'brrp' that I turned round. He was just sitting there looking at me. A metre away. He had huge yellow eyes."

"All the better to size you up, young man. For a meal. Or worse, just for fun."

"Honestly Gwynneth, I swear he was trying to talk to me."

"Stop carrying on and sip your sap" Gwyneth commanded.

"I really thought he wanted to say something. I might go back and try to find him tomorrow."

"Oh Gerry, you are such a dear sweet boy. It will get you eaten."

Gerry concentrated on sliding his thin green rostrum into the soft wood to draw out some lovely sap. He recognised the crisp fragrant taste of a lemon-scented gum.

"We may have a visit from Cir Franklin after dinner." Garth said to Gerry, lifting his rostrum out from the sweet sap for a minute.

He pronounced it correctly, 'Sir', but all cicadas knew it was spelled with a 'C'.

Some said it stood for 'Cicada In Readiness'. Some thought it was 'Cicada in Regalia'.

Someone once suggested "Chief in Resonance".

All of those would actually apply quite admirably to Cir Franklin.

"Gwyneth met him in the Park today apparently. She asked him over."

"That's a high honour, isn't it? Him coming here."
"Oh yes, Cir Franklin doesn't just fly in any window" said George.

"What other windows could he fly through? Aren't we the only cicadas to own a building in the city?"

"We are as far as I know, smartypants."

A scrape of a shoe on the wooden floor had them frozen for a second. The three of them looked up quickly. Cicadas are understandably nervous of sudden movements, although you wouldn't know it because they don't fling themselves about like startled flies. Gerry, Garth and George relaxed as they recognised the young man in the white lab coat. He was tidying the table and pulling out a few more branches from the centre to the edge for a couple of Black Princes and a

Cherrynose who had just flown in.

The Greengrocers nodded politely at the newcomers who were very young and sleek. One of them produced a quick chirrup on his drums when he saw the delicious branches. His screech, while not nearly as loud as a Greengrocer in full song - it was more of a high pitched buzz - reverberated in the quiet room. The others looked up though they were much too polite to say anything; but as the Cherrynose looked around the room his innate sense of decency, well-developed even in one so young, brought a shy apology.

Gerry turned to the young man in the white coat who turned towards him with a smile.

"This is lemon-scented isn't it?"

"Yes, Gerry, *eucalyptus citriodora*. You prefer that don't you?"

"Not all the time. I like to try them all. I don't think there are any I don't like."

"You know there are over nine hundred species of eucalyptus don't you?"

"Will I get to try them all?"

The young man's eyes clouded a little, then he brightened up and smiled again. It was a most interesting smile. He had quite a long face with a deep pointed chin, like a goblet holding the volume of his mouth with his teeth at the brim. He had good straight teeth, always on display.

His smile was straight across, very broad and very genuine. His eyes behind his large rimless aviator lenses almost always smiled. Even his father, a most unsentimental man, often said that Merac had a "kind smile".

"We'll try to get through them all, Gerry. I'll bring you a couple of new ones tomorrow and we'll give it our best shot."

Of all people, Dr Meracanthus Matrices, Professor of Insectry at the University of East Sydney, knew that none of the cheerful little creatures around his table could live to savour every eucalyptus. Even if he brought them only the species of eucalypts which he could comfortably access in the Sydney area, on one a day they would not get through them.

He crouched down to Gerry's level.

"Tell me some more about this cat."

"I saw him in a laneway across the Park. I was on top of a brick wall ..."

"That was silly."

"I know I know, I wasn't singing. I was only there for a second, moving onto another tree. This house has a big gum in the back. I suppose the cat lives in there. He just appeared behind me. I had to admire his skill. Big, big cat. Black as a nymph's burrow. He was standing when I turned, then he sat. He 'brrrped' at me. 'Brrrp. Brrrrrrp'. A few times. Different each time. As though he was speaking. Not quite a purr, but a question. You know?"

"I know cats."

"Should I go back?"

"I wouldn't. But I know I can't stop you. At least check him out from a thin branch next time."

They both turned to the open window as they heard a bit of a commotion which seemed to come from the building next door.

A girl was screaming.

"Get it out! Get it out!"

"It's only a cicada, calm down. I'll get it." A young male voice reassured her.

More screaming. Then a rich and vibrant squawking sound. Panicky but defiant. A flutter of wings into the outside air.

"Is it gone?"

"Yes, it's gone"

"What was it?"

"If you'd grown up in Sydney you would have recognised it. A Floury Baker. Or it might have been a Double Drummer. A male. You can tell by the noise."

All the cicadas in Merac's room recognised the 'noise" and winced at the description.

Noise? Noise? Please!

The *Song* if you don't mind. The deep and glorious song of the baritone of the cicadas' choir.

A few seconds later, composed and unruffled, Cir Franklin shot through the open window, hovered and took his place on the central pile of branches.

"Touch of excitement there. Wrong window, what. Gwynneth must have described it wrongly.

Can't be helped. Well here we are. Please be seated everyone."

"We are seated," whispered Gerry to George who tried not to find him amusing. "We just look like we're standing."

Cir Franklin continued. "Mind if I have a slurp before we start. Wet my whistle. It's a tad further than I thought from the Park and I had to do a spot of evasive action in front of the Library. Those pigeons are usually too slow but one of these days they might just breed a smart one."

Gerry wondered what this noble guest had come to talk about. He hoped it was something adventurous. A quest perhaps. He'd love a quest. He had a small one of his own planned for tomorrow.

There was a brief conversation between Merac, Gwynneth and Cir Franklin.

Sitting close by, Gerry heard him outline his thoughts. Something about bringing humans and inanimate objects together in harmony. What are *they,* wondered Gerry. Cir Franklin illustrated his points with a couple of jolly anecdotes. Merac and Gwynneth were nodding.

Finally the senior cicada told them he wanted to reschedule his presentation.

He was concerned at the small numbers currently in the room. It was agreed that there would be another meeting after they had had a chance to sing the word around.

Cir Franklin would return tonight to a packed house.

Chapter Four

In the middle of Tim's bed was a grey cat.

He was curled up so tightly you couldn't see where his head or tail was.

At a casual glance he looked like one of those Russian fur hats.

You'd wonder if he could possibly make himself any smaller.

The cat's name was Theodore Edward Dexter. Ted. He was a Blue British Shorthair. He should have been much larger, with a really boofy face and the fat cheek pouches typical of the breed. But Ted was almost delicate. He was the runt of his litter and, now thirteen years old, he seemed to be shrinking even smaller. He slept almost all of the day and even nighttimes were not much of a buzz for him anymore. He rarely roamed. The creatures of the night, the mice, the birds, the lizards, the moths he'd terrorised in the past were no longer of interest to him. It was hard to tell what was of interest to him. He would often just sit and look at things as though he had forgotten what to do. He would adopt strange locations to sleep for three of four days in a row and then move on. As though he had forgotten where the good cat spots were. Dad and Mum thought Ted may be developing dementia.

He had developed a weakness in his back legs and often missed his jumps. At his best gallop he now ran with his back legs crabbing sideways. He could only go in short bursts because his back would overtake his front and he would end up facing where he started.

"Definitely on his last legs." said Mum.

"I believe those are his first legs too." said Dad.

But Tim who had always believed Ted was more his cat than anyone else's stood up for him.

"He's ninety one years old. I bet when you're in your nineties you'll hit your chin and miss when you try to jump onto the table. "

"Maybe I won't try."

"I bet you will because now I've dared you. I'll be waiting."

'That's quite a way away, mate."

"You'll probably run sideways too. I'll be watching you carefully over the next few years. I never forget you know."

Mum had found the trunk. The shoebox was in the bottom of it. She didn't know why she hadn't looked into everything in the first place. Her eye had been caught by the pretty purse with her sister's first driving licence and a few other things including the 'idea for a story.' She had been so taken with that, she'd gone to find Dad without going through everything else. She had thought they were just a pile of uninteresting papers that could wait for some other time.

Now she came up to Dad holding some of those papers.

"She had a baby. Two years before she died. A girl."

"What?"

"My sister had a baby. She gave her up for adoption."

"Wow."

"It looks like she came up to Sydney for the birth. We were here and she didn't even contact us. Oh god, what she must have gone through. All by herself. She must have been hoping no one back home found out. Hoping she wouldn't bump into us. And then no baby. Oh poor Sis."

Mum ran her fingers up through her hair. Dad could see the eyes moistening and put his arm around her shoulders.

"Can I have a look at those?"

Mum let him take them gently. She leant into him.

"Does it say where the baby is now?"

"No. None of that. I just assume someone in this town now has a seven year old girl sharing some of my DNA."

"Father's details?"

"Unknown."

"I suppose he never knew about it. She must've wanted to keep it from him, if she came up here. He can't have been a man she wanted to be with."

"It's so sad. She never told me. Now she never will."

"Do you think those words on that paper have something to do with this?"

"How do you mean?"

"I dunno. A lost girl with the same initials. Could be a story she made up to ... um ... make up for losing the child."

Mum took back the papers.

"I want to find out more. Is that OK with you?"

"Sure."

"Sure?

As Ted slumbered, a big black cat rose slowly on his back legs, effortlessly resting its paws on the top covers to check the sleeping Blue in the middle of the bed. He thought of going there himself but dropped down again and set off for a spot in the garden. He was also a British Shorthair, four years old. He did have a huge boofy face and a solid well-rounded body. His fur was startlingly sleek and glossy. His eyes were flawless orbs of yellow gold. He was like a jaguar, an exceptional feline. Exceptional in looks and power. The creatures of the night had many years of fear ahead of them. Even people who didn't like cats were impressed at his appearance. He was almost too heavy to pick up. Cat lovers always walked straight to him for a pat and a stroke, and a chuckle of his chubby cheeks. He knew he was a handsome boy and he loved it.

His name was Montgomery Obsidian Newton Tewksbury Yarmouth.

Everybody called him Monty.

Nobody knew he had a secret.

Chapter Five

Macquarie Street is Sydney's most important and attractive thoroughfare.

Down the Eastern side from Hyde Park, The Barracks, The Mint, Parliament House, Sydney Hospital, the Library, the Gardens, right down to the Opera House it combines old with new. Beauty with power.

In the streets on the other side towards The Quay there are many concrete, steel and glass towers.

It would be hard to imagine any sort of family living in there with their cavernous marble foyers, gleaming lift banks and 24 hour blaze of lights.

You couldn't imagine Dad sitting opposite at a bus stop sketching and dreaming.

Cicadas are not fond of them either. There are terrible slipstreams and windshears around their smooth exteriors and there is never an open window to pop into and catch up with friends.

This is where people fight for the celebrated views. This is the smart part of Sydney. At least it is thought so by the people who daily occupy these wonderfully sited spaces. The most important people fight to gain a corner office. They may have to make do with the carpet they are given but they make a case for Persian rugs, mahogany desks and Whiteleys on the wall. They have wonderful views through their floor to ceiling glass windows all the way down the Harbour to the Heads.

The closer they are to Macquarie Street the better their view of the Botanic Gardens and the Opera House. These spaces are important. Not because the occupants need the actual space, their daily business is often conducted in physical simplicity with their bum on a seat and their ear to a phone, but the magnificence of these eyries confers respect. Nobody except the regulars can walk into one of these offices without commenting on the view. Rain or shine it is still spectacular, and visitors feel a twinge, however slight or grudging, of respect for its occupant.

For the first time visitor, the view can be quite moving especially for someone who has known the Harbour only from water level. A significant change of altitude has always given humans a buzz they can't explain.

Even if you are a custodian of decent but lesser views from a building a few blocks down the ridge, it is appropriate to be impressed. It may be simple envy. But for the many schemers who inhabit this patch of town it can be a caution. 'Who does this bastard know that I don't? I'd better be careful.'

Among the occupants of one of these top level eyries, was the Director for the Control of the Environment.

His office was in a towering green glass building overlooking the Botanic Gardens. That verdant crescent of two hundred years of managed vegetation was on show daily to those in the building who cared to study it. It filled the bottom half of his windows, above that the scalloping shores of the Harbour worked their way towards the Heads. Above that, the sky kept itself clear and clean with ocean breezes. From this vantage point it was simply beautiful.

Harold Scortz was not a minister in the Government, although he had been earlier in his career. His current position, due to his previous responsibilities, contacts and clashes, carried even more weight in the real business of the city than his last appointment as Minister for Gaming Enhancement, a portfolio abolished, or rather folded into one of the other financial ministries shortly after he stepped down.

His assistant, Paul Wrightray, an English chap of quite good breeding but previously questionable alliances, stood by checking his watch as The Boss finished his phone conversation.

"No, no, no, maaaate, no! You don't do it yourself, mate. You pay a couple of blokes to find a couple of Maoris down at the pub. They know how to do it. They drill a few holes, in goes half a bucket of Roundup and Bob's your uncle. The tree dies, council has to take it away and your view comes back. Adds a few hundred thou to the value of your house."

Paul checked his watch again.

"No worries, Doc. Always a pleasure. Playing Saturday? Yep. See ya."

Harold had no eyes for the view; it was just water and trees to him. He knew that Paul standing quietly meant he was due to do some work. He always loved that.

"Paul, my little wildflower. Stop posing like a lily and bring them in. Who are they by the way?"

"The Friends of the City Trees. Meg Musgrave and Robertson Mooney. You know her, I believe. A Mosman lady. One of your neighbours, perhaps?"

"Oh her. Bloody Meg. This'll be a riot. Who's the bloke?"

"Robertson Mooney OBE"

"Aargh. One of them. Old money. Money old enough to buy a gong from Her Maj. Is he a shirt lifter?"

"I'm sure I don't know what you mean."

"Sorry, precious. Bring 'em in. Interrupt us in ten, OK? Say it's the Minister, right?"

"As you wish."

There could not be a much greater contrast in any two voices speaking the English language. Roger Moore and a Brixton navvy perhaps. Paul's modulations were understated Home Counties, rounded but not excessive. Harold was more chainsaw with nasal vowels British masters of the language are fond of mimicking, and the flat delivery that leads many Americans to believe they can say "The dingo took my baby" to hilarious perfection, they were Harold's hallmarks.

Up and down Macquarie Street, Paul and Harold were known as a strange pair but no one took them head on and said as much to their faces. Individually they were quite influential. Bound together by the sheets of dirty laundry they had on each other, they were a serious combination behind any closed doors. Not many could stand up to being on their wrong side for long. Unfortunately they made it their business to be on everybody's wrong side as soon as possible. That was their pleasure.

"Meg, jeez you're looking good"

He dropped a kiss on her hand holding it tightly in his ginger-haired lump of a paw.

Oh My God, thought Robertson. He had only a spilt second to feel disgusted before the other hand was stuck out for him to shake, even while Harold was still slobbering on poor Meg.

"G'day, Roland. Nice to meetcha."

"It's Robertson, actually."

"Course it is. Grab a seat. Paul'll be in with the drinks in a mo. What can I do for you people today?"

The sun was setting somewhere off behind the city towers as they slid in to the wonderfully comfortable chairs facing the desk where Harold was now perched. Good Lord, thought Robertson. It's actually on a platform.

To their left and behind them the windows of other buildings facing the sun were lighting up in yellow and the harbour waters were taking on their own sheen of gold.

"Harold."

"Meg."

"We've come to you because, quite frankly, some of your colleagues …"

"Former colleagues."

"…are being less than helpful."

"Why am I not surprised."

"Our organisation is as you know interested in all the trees in the city of Sydney, but we have particular concerns about the ones in some of the less well known parks. Hyde Park of course we understand the need for… um … lopping and replanting. Sad but it must be done. Although you can be sure we will remain forever vigilant. The Domain was a great pity. Quite poorly handled we thought. Those poor trees. The measures that were eventually taken we believe were not necessary. It is hard to imagine anyone who took those decisions having the well-being of this city and its trees at heart. We thought we were speaking to the right people. We followed all the procedures, addressed the right committees over many months while the poor trees were suffering. Robertson, God bless him, even called in a few favours and offered some better outcomes through negotiation. Money was being raised. We were assured at the highest level we were being listened to and whoosh ... it all went wrong. It was as though some ... some maniac had stepped in at the last minute."

"They're a tough bunch Meg. Can't trust some of them."

"What we are hoping for, and this report spells out in some detail the parks and the individual trees we are seeking protection for, is an assurance that the city's many Small Parks will be afforded the same kind of protection, in perpetuity, that is enjoyed by what we hold as the Crown Jewels, the Botanic Gardens."

"Simple enough request, Meg. Very understandable. Very reasonable. You make your points well."

God, what a disgusting man thought Robertson as he followed Harold's eyes and, yes, they were on Meg's chest. Meg, in her fifties was not beautiful and never had been, but "handsome" could be easily applied. Her family's money ensured she was well looked after, not least in a cosmetic sense. She had strong features, well framed with insistent black hair. She carried well a large but still athletic figure. Her last fancy dress ball had seen her dressed very effectively as Wonderwoman. They played tennis at her house on weekends and as an occasional guest Roberson had certainly noticed her tightly and no doubt expensively brassiered bosom surging proudly across the clipped grass.

Meg continued on. Even if Robertson had pointed out the grubbiness of that remark later on she would not have believed that anyone could be so ... so awful in open forum.

"So Harold, we are depending on you to a large extent. Our small parks are the petite lungs of this beautiful city of ours, and we must ensure they continue to breathe clean and deeply. I'll leave this report with you. And we'll hear from you, shortly?"

"Course you will. Is that it?"

"Short and sweet." Robertson offered, now feeling like a cleansing swim in the surf.

"We'll get on with it then." Harold rose and held out his hand again. Robertson noticed the cufflink was a golden bunch of grapes.

The grip was stronger this time. Harold had sized up the physicality of his visitor. He must be ten years older, but he has the build of a boxer. A class or two up in weight than me. A Gentleman Jim to my Raging Bull. I can take him anytime, Harold thought.

The grins and gripping persisted until Meg noticed. Her husband had told her of Harold's handshakes being a sore point around town. Feeling breezy and girlish, after all the meeting had gone well, she switched on the smile that brought most men to heel.

"Harold, you put Robertson down. Pick on someone your own size."

With the meeting more or less at an end, Meg asked to use the ladies room. Harold instantly directed her, not to the dedicated female toilet out in the hallway, but to his private ensuite. That was exactly what she had hoped for. She had no real need to go but she had heard, as her beloved Guide Michelin might say, the view from this loo was well worth a detour or even worth a special journey.

Paul came back into the boardroom and hovered in the window looking fondly East. Robertson moved to join him. Soundlessly, Harold just appeared behind him.

He rapped on Robertson's arm like a doorknock.

"Lovely views from here eh, Roger? Worth squillions. The higher the better. If this block was apartments you'd easy add a mill each floor you go up. If it was on the other side of Macquarie Street right on top of the Gardens, you could double that again. Right on the water, where that stone wall is running round, triple it. I tell a lie, quadruple it. Good at arithmetic, are you Roger? How many apartments do ya reckon you could fit in there. From there to there. Go on, have a guess."

Harold's fat mitt swung through forty five degrees, from the Opera House to Mrs Macquarie's Chair.

Robertson followed the rough gesture with distaste. After some time in the army, straight from school to Military College at Duntroon, he had made his career with ASIO, seconded for periods to both the CIA and MI5, and had met some very evil men in his time. It was plainly because of what he had seen and what he had done, that he now devoted the energy of the later part of his life to good works. He wasn't a pussycat; he had been violently tough in his early days as a spook but he was basically an honest and decent man in a slippery profession who at the end had been relieved to get out. He left early but with a good record. If he had demonstrated an ongoing liking for dirty tricks he could have had another five years and a knighthood.

His instincts told him that the jolly chunk of a man beside him was a nastier piece of work than anyone he'd met in the underworld of Sydney and possibly even in the alleys of Brazzaville, Baghdad, or Belgrade.

"Do you know the number yourself?"

"Come off it, Rollo. I'm not allowed to do those kind of sums." Harold chortled with a broad smile that showed very expensive teeth. "Course not. Government would never allow it. Sacred ground, that is. They'd have my guts for garters if I ever suggested it. However one quiet afternoon Paul and I did pass a bit of time looking out the window with the calculator. Nearly broke the bastard."

"So you know?"

"Very rough number."

"Four hundred." guessed Robertson.

"Total? You're joking! Nearly that many in a single block. We could do ten blocks! Average three million bucks. Penthouses twenty mill."

"That's a lot."

"You'd hardly have to knock down any trees."

Robertson turned sharply. Harold beamed at him. Flash as a rat with a gold tooth.

"That gotcha. Got to learn to take a joke, Ronnie."

Harold turned away from the view he'd built on many times in his mind.

He walked through the Gardens some days, staying to the paths, careful not to take his black crocodile skin slipons onto the moist grass. The shoes he had made to order in London. Years ago he'd seen a magazine article about a cat burglar who lifted the jewels of the International set on the French Riviera in the sixties and seventies. It mentioned that this gentleman villain who was never caught bought his shoes at this venerated bootmaker in the West End. That was good enough for Harold.

On his walks in the Gardens he had counted which trees would have to go. Those two rotten old bastards overlooking the Opera House first. Harold chuckled at Robertson's shocked face. He can turn up his nose all he likes. Imperial orders might mean something in Mosman but this is the big city.

"Yeah. Fun way to fill in an arvo. Paul's idea of course. He carries the calculator around here."

Robertson looked out at the view again.

He thought Sydney's a lovely city but it's a tough town.

After they left, Harold came back to find Paul, who

41

was ready to pour a glass of wine.

The meeting had been so swift that they hadn't even had time to share a drink with their visitors. Paul eased the cork on a John Riddoch, Harold's favourite red, 'any vintage will do, as long as it's old and expensive.'

"List of jobs for tomorrow, my old fruit. Ask the blokes over the road if they have any form on Mr OBE and get onto the city people and find out just how much real estate around this town is actually locked up under Small Parks and Gardens."

Chapter Six

The Sydney Red Gum is not a real gum tree. It isn't a eucalypt. It's an angophora, a close cousin.

Each year when the old bark peels off a Sydney Red, the new bark is a cheerful orangey colour turning dusky pink. It is wonderfully smooth and warm to the touch under a hot sun. The trunk feels solid of course but somehow contains the promise of juiciness inside.

On a big old tree the random wanderings of the branches produce many swollen joints like folds at the elbows of a thick sweater. In them you can see a deeper redness. There will probably be a couple of jagged grey stumps where branches have broken off and dropped. Like many Australian trees it prunes itself when it hasn't sufficient water.

On a young tree, you can see the nascent redness in the spindly branches, with the leaves, red at birth, turning dark green against a hot blue sky.

On a tree of any age you can see bright burgundy immediately you pierce the skin and the sap oozes thickly and sets like garnet glass. This tree grows happily on outcrops of Hawkesbury sandstone, the base rock of the geological region that most of the metropolis is built on. It often wraps its roots around slabs of stone for stability. There are a still number of pure stands around Sydney's coastline, and sometimes you'll find a survivor in the city or suburbs.

The true eucalypts, the River Red Gum and the Forest Red Gum will be found further inland. Sturdy, straight and massive with a splendid red timber inside, they are nonetheless grey and formal on the outside with grey green leaves. They tend to be sober stoic stockers of forests, unlike their colourful city cousins.

Melbourne people would say it's 'so Sydney' to produce something flamboyant but phoney to upstage the real thing.

A very pretty example of a Sydney Red Gum grew in the backyard of Tim's house in Yurong Street, close to the brick wall near the back lane. It was mid-sized and nicely shaped, like a slender forearm topped by a hand with fingers formed into a goblet. Like most native trees it was more air than timber. Looking up at it you would see as much blue sky as branches and leaves. Aussie kids learn to draw trees not with a thick ball of green on top of a brown stump like European trees, but with a series of wobbly brown strokes upward from a central trunk each with a squiggle of green leaves at its end.

One of the lower branches of Tim's tree passed close to the top of the brick wall. On the thinnest part of the branch hidden in its bunch of leaves Gerry Greengrocer sat still and breathless. On the dusky pink trunk he would stand out, in the leaves he was almost invisible. His claws dug lightly into the warm bark, savouring the perpetual motion of the swaying wind. Much of a cicada's activities involve the unmoving trunks of trees, but they really enjoy the rhythms of nature, the updrafts of the air they fly in and the wind's persistence expressed in the movement of upper branches.

Gerry could do with a suck of sap after his flight from the Park, but he didn't want to put his head down. His eyes, all five of them, scanned the wall and what he could see of the yard.

Like all cicadas he had a pair of large eyes either side of his head. His were a soft glossy brown against the vibrant lime colour of his face. His vision was quite good for several metres. He could detect all but very slow movement. He also had what his friends called 'jewels', his ocelli, a group of three pinpoint dots arranged in a triangular pattern in the middle of his head, right between the large eyes. These had less to do with direct vision but helped him lock on to sources of light such as the sun or the moon which was important to his navigation when flying.

Gerry had been sitting for an hour. The movement of the branch and the warmth of the sun were putting him to sleep. His head was full of thoughts about what Cir Franklin might say tonight. He had spoken to Merac who gave him some hints about the Quest and something to do with 'things that were unhappy'. He wasn't quite sure because he couldn't stop his mind wandering to the possibility of meeting the cat again and the prospect of tasting the dozens of varieties of delicious sap Professor Merac had promised him. He knew which of those he'd prefer, but he'd set himself a small mission. A quest is a quest and he had to get on with it.

Only a very few cicadas, and Gerry was one of them, have a tendency to daydream and think too much about the future. They are mostly very pragmatic and energetic, disposed to take direct action. They know they have little time for a contemplative life.

He thought about his adventure today, another

meeting with the cat. If it all went well it would give him a little more experience to speak up at tonight's meeting. After all, cats were closely associated with humans and humans knew more than cicadas about 'things' so a meeting with a cat might produce some valuable insights to help him participate in Cir Franklin's quest.

"Brrrp. Brrrrrrrp"

Gerry froze. It sounded like a roar in his ears. How close *is* that!

Monty, less than a metre away could not see that Gerry had frozen. Gerry sitting happily daydreaming and Gerry frozen with fear looked exactly the same to him. And Monty's eyesight was very good.

Gerry turned to face the noise. A cicada obviously cannot turn its head, so it took two seconds for Gerry to wheel his body on his six thinly jointed legs. The big black cat was on the wall just below him.

How did he do that! I didn't see him at all. How can he move so quickly and quietly, a big fella like that?

Gerry looked down into the black face. The eyes that had fixed on him were as big as a double sunset on an African plain. Huge golden pools he could almost fall into.

In the moments he stared at the vertical slits in the unblinking orbs Gerry detected an intelligence, a fellow thinker, perhaps a daydreamer, certainly an appreciator of fine food, a gourmet even, judging by the size of the beast.

"Come on down, sport."

As easy as that, he heard the cat talking to him.

"Come on. I won't hurt you."

"Your kind usually do."

"You're dead right about that. But I'm not a usual kind of cat. And you're not a usual kind of cicada."

"That's true. Could you move over a little."

Gerry fluttered down. He landed badly, but recovered quickly. Cicadas are not precision flyers over short distances. Bricks are hard to hold onto. He walked up to where the cat was sitting. This was a big moment indeed.

Gerry had trouble looking up at the height of the cat. The cat recognised that and took four paces to where the wall stepped down a couple of bricks. He dropped down silently and turned with a fluid sweep of his tail to settle with his eyes close to Gerry's level. Gerry marched quickly and stiffly the way cicadas do to face him again.

"The name's Monty. Headbutt?"

"My name is Gerry. What?"

"Headbutt. Tim calls them headbutts. I'll show you." The cat lowered his head and pushed towards Gerry.

It was never going to work. His nose and chin were scraping.

Monty sized him up again and twisted his head on one side brushing his chubby cheek along the warm bricks to bring his forehead up to Gerry's. The poor cicada was engulfed in a mass of warm black fur. It all went dark for a minute, but there was no solid contact.

Monty pulled back and began to laugh.

"Not going to work is it? We'll have to think of another way to say g'day. Shame about that; the headbutt's become a bit of a tradition in our family."

"You live here?"

"All six of us. Nine with the fish. It was ten yesterday but one died. They have such sad lives, poor little buggers. Round and round. Forget everything. Then you die. Mum said she's not replacing this one. Those other three are on their last legs."

"Fish? I'm not sure I've ever seen one. They have legs?"

49

"Only last ones."

"Who are the six."

"Dad, Mum, Ellie, Tim, Ted and me."

"Are you all the same age?"

"Dad's really old. He can remember black and white television. I can never see what they see in television. Mum's next, then Ted, Ellie, Tim and me. That's actual years, but the humans multiply our years by seven to compare our ages with theirs."

"Why is that?"

"Because we don't live as long."

"That's interesting. There's something about seven years in a cicada's life. I'm not sure what it is. I wasn't paying attention when Gwynneth was telling us. I'll have to ask her later."

"Do you live very long?"

"No. We mostly get eaten in the first few days."

"Shame, that. Not that there's anything wrong with eating. You just don't want it to happen to you."

"By birds mostly, then cats."

"Ted'd eat you. He's a nice cat, quite a gentleman actually, but he eats most moving things smaller than himself. How long do you live if you don't get eaten?"

"I don't know. I've never done this before. The

cicadas that were here when I arrived don't talk about it much. Seems to be something they don't like discussing. But Professor Merac gave me a clue the other day; I think it might not be very long."

"We'd have to multiply your age by ten or twelve then."

"Maybe even more."

They heard a noise in the garden below. In spite of his soft paws and slow pace Ted could not help the scratch and crunch his feet made in the dried leaves on the paving. Gerry couldn't see over the edge of the wall but it was a new sound to him and his instincts told him to be wary. It was not the weaving of the breeze to which he was well attuned. He began to walk backwards, preparing for take off. Monty gave him a nod and looked over the edge. He gave a low growl. Then a couple of flat nasal sounds, very soft, almost lost in the breeze. 'Yeow. Yow'.

Ted heard them and understood. He turned and walked to a sunny spot on the other side of the backyard. Gerry could now see him as he hopped onto a low border wall around a garden bed.

"That's how you talk to each other. What did you say?"

51

"Told him this was none of his business. He understands. We go our own ways most of the day. We eat together. Not the same bowl. Mine's the big one. We might share the occasional rub, lick or headbutt. That's about it. We sleep side by side in winter in front of the heater. Ted snores. Ellie laughs, but Tim sticks up for him, and reminds her how old he really is."

"Do you like ... er, get on well with your humans? Do you know what they talk about?" Gerry was angling for a snip or two of information, a good quote even, that he could take to tonight's discussion.

"Can you understand what they are saying?"

"Too right." Monty rose to stretch, arching then bowing. His stretch as always included a wide-mouthed yawn, exposing a set of needle-pointed fangs set in healthy pink gums. Shivering slowly and satisfyingly, he held the end position extracting the maximum enjoyment and then resettled with his eyes even closer to Gerry. Gerry flinched. All his instincts, everything he had ever been told, even the Professor's gentle warning was giving him tingles in his wings. He was within a flutter of getting out of there. Onto a thin branch at least. Maybe he could tell Monty he was feeling too hot in the sun, that he needed to be in the shade of the leaves.

But the golden globes were pure and free of malice.

"Too right we understand. They can't understand us. Although I sometimes reckon Tim's getting the hang of it. I don't think he knows specific words, but he picks up on inflections. Much more than the rest of the family. The people next door have one of those yappy little dogs and I've seen Tim trying to talk to her, but she's not easy."

Monty was enjoying this rare stationary audience and rattled on.

"Yap Yap Yap. What could that mean! He perseveres with us cats. I think he reads Ted better than me, but that's sweet, I know Ted's his favourite. The fish are bloody hopeless. Even if you knew their language you couldn't make it out through all that water.

They speak with their mouths full. Do you like water? Terrible stuff. I'm told fish can only remember two words at a time. That's what water does to you. They have to relearn everything every lap of their pool. Except swimming. That stays with them."

Monty's conversation was charming, wandering

and time wasting. An endless flow of words from an intelligent, indolent gentleman totally supported by his family. Just like many British chaps throughout the history of this colony.

Gerry was mesmerised. Unusually for a cicada he could have happily sat for hours in the sun, just listening to the words of this new creature and drifting in his own mind with the thoughts they provoked. But he was still a cicada and he knew he had to get on with things.

All cicadas share the feeling that just behind them, where their eyes can not reach, time is a shadow pressing forward to engulf them. Not as simple as the shadow of the sun moving across the earth. That can be observed and understood. Their Time Shadow can not be seen. It can be felt just behind the periphery of their vision, and they know it is approaching every day. They have a joke that goes : " if a cicada could turn its head suddenly…" It's not much of a joke.

The shadow of time drives them all their waking moments, which is *all* of their moments, because they don't actually sleep.

"Do your humans have any concerns that are not World Peace or Global Warming?"

"What!"

Monty was amused by this small person. He raised his right foreleg over the step of the wall and pushed it towards Gerry with the carefree approach he would take to any small thing that took his attention. Unfortunately this movement also included an involuntary opening of the paw.

At the full arm extension, curved claws as sharp as a surgeon's needles unsheathed from the chubby black pads, a sight more frightening to Gerry than the teeth that had scared him a minute ago.

Gerry stood his ground, his wings tingling like tuning forks.

Monty relaxed his paw into a pillow of furry comfort which nudged Gerry's wiry little legs.

"Now what kind of question is that, sport?"

Gerry was flustered. He didn't know that his cicada's directness would be out of place in a lazy top-of-the-wall conversation. But he pushed on, conscious of the sun slipping down another notch or two in the blue sky. He was still concerned at having nothing much thing to offer at the meeting.

"Do they have any things that bother them? Not big things but little things. Things that little people might help with."

"Little people like you. Where did this all come from?"

"Some of us were wondering if we could help. The humans, that is. You cats don't seem to need help. You seem to be doing alright, if I may say so."

Gerry flinched as Monty could not help stretching his claws along the bricks as he listened. He *was* happy. A cat on a hot brick wall.

"Indeed yes, life is good for most cats most of the time."

"Our senior cicada says the World at Large is not happy. But there is not a lot we cicadas can do about it even though we want to. He said the really big worries like World Peace and Global Warming were being looked after by others better qualified ... Miss Universe and Greenpeas. Do you know them?"

"I've heard of them."

"Cir Franklin is going to ask us to come up with something that may help the humans in some small way. Is there anything small your humans are unhappy with?"

"They seem to be very happy with each other. And with us, needless to say. Ted and I are the masters at keeping them onside. Even if I get into the garbage bin at night, spread a few chicken bones around or leave a dead mouse under the table, I can charm them with a few leg rubs. A plaintive meaow or brrrrp, which is actually not part of the vocabulary Ted and I use to speak to each other, can have them thinking we are so cute that we're off the hook. It works every time."

"So what are their problems, apart from ... scheming cats?"

"You're not a bad little schemer yourself." Monty ran his tongue around a smile, appraising his guest, before continuing.

"Problems? Problems? Let me think. I'd reckon Dad has the most problems when he's working on the house. Judging by the swearing, which, to be fair, he only does outside the house or when the family isn't there. What upsets him most are the things in his toolbox, or the things around the house that the things in his toolbox are working on."

"Such as?"

"A screw. Or the screwdriver. A hammer. A piece of wire. A lump of wood. A saw. A pencil. A brick. They do something he isn't expecting, something he doesn't like and he swears at them. He shouts at them sometimes, and screams things like 'Why the bloody hell did you do that?' "

"Do these things tell him why they did it?"

"No. They can't. It doesn't stop him asking though. More accusing than asking. I've seen him almost blue in the face. He apologised to me once. 'Pardon my French' he said, when I was sitting next to him the day he dropped a screw down the plug hole. I think some of his anger might be rubbing off on the boy, too. Tim was very cranky with a piece of toast the other day. He doesn't swear, of course, but he was very tight lipped and asked why it *always* falls buttered side down. I thought he was going to stamp his foot. He might've, if the toast hadn't been right there."

Gerry felt a tingle of excitement. He phrased his next sentence carefully and delivered it slowly, like a question from a prosecuting barrister. He hoped Cir Franklin would be proud.

"Would you say … these things that upset them … were …'inanimate objects'?"

"You've hit the nail on the head. That's just what they are."

"Ah, that's interesting. Cir Franklin and Merac think 'things' by which they mean 'inanimate objects' might be part of the world problem. He says humans are often frustrated by inanimate objects, but they can't improve the situation because they don't know inanimate objects have feelings too. Humans never listen to them. But Cir Franklin does. He was talking to a nail the other day and it told him it was really bored with holding up a wall. It wanted to go surfing."

"How does a nail know about surfing?"

"It can watch the sports channel from where it is."

"He also mentioned a rock he'd been told about in the Botanic Gardens that wanted to sail a boat. This nice piece of sandstone has seen everything that's sailed in Sydney Harbour since before the First Fleet came in. All it wants is a chance to go sailing. But of course no sailor would think of taking that rock on board. For a start, how does any sailor know that the rock *wants* to go sailing."

"Don't know a lot about sailors, but I reckon you're spot on."

"Cir Franklin was saying last night that maybe if inanimate objects and humans understood each other better there might be some more harmony in the world."

"Sir Franklin is your … senior cicada?"

"That's right."

"Sounds like a very astute bloke. He's putting all this together, isn't he? Is that why he sent you?"

"No, I came here by myself. I thought you might help me."

"So, let's run through the links in this chain. Sir Franklin says he can talk to inanimate objects; he can also talk to you. You can talk to me and I can tell you what humans are saying. You can take that back to Sir Franklin and he can talk to the nail or the rock. Is that what you had in mind?"

"Not until I came here. It only occurred to me when you started talking about Dad and the plug hole."

"Maybe you're the astute one, eh."

"It's just an idea but do you think we could work something out?"

"Sure. Tell your boss what you've heard today. Who knows where it could lead. There might be something in it for all of us."

"I think I'll discuss it with the Professor Merac first. Cir Franklin can be quite intimidating if you don't have all your arguments well marshalled. He spends a lot of time around the Law Courts apparently. The Prof is very patient with young cicadas. I'm sure he'll help me."

"Does your Professor live round here?"

"He works just up the road at the University of East Sydney. He lives over on Phillip Street."

"Where's that?"

"Right over the Park then down a few blocks."

"Never been there. Just Avoca where I was born. I can hardly recall it, but I've heard Mum and Dad talk about it. All I know is this small stretch of Yurong Street including Yurong Lane where we're sitting now, where I now live."

"We have dinner and our meetings in the Professor's house. It *must* be his house, although he insists it belongs to us. Well, I'd better be getting back now."

"Before you go, tell me some more about the noise you make. I hear a lot of you from the Park most evenings and also in some of the trees in these streets round here. I've got a good ear, and reckon I can detect at least five different sounds. Is that it?"

"For a start, we don't call it noise, we call it song. You say you recognise five? The Professor tells us there are dozens of different ones all around the country. But if you're talking Sydney, that's pretty close. Basically we Greengrocers are somewhere in the middle of the singing range. The Prof says we are the tenors. Our close cousins the Chocolate Soldiers and the Yellow Mondays are also tenors. It's hard to tell us apart, but we can. We have the loudest song. It comes from these drums right down here, see there, the Prof calls them tymbals. We vibrate them really fast. It doesn't sound at all like a drum, more like a brassy shriek. The Prof said we can reach 120 decibels and we can hurt a human ear. A group of us singing at full volume can actually drive birds away. They must have sensitive ears too. Would 120 decibels hurt your eardrums?"

Monty nodded with a flick of his furry tipped ears. "Too right they would. What are the other songs?"

"Much deeper than us are the Double Drummers. They're bigger so it's really a matter of size: they sing baritone and bass and their song is a sort of rhythmic rumble. If you go down by the water you'll hear a higher pitched steady squeal which comes from the Black Princes and Cherry Noses, they are the sopranos. The Floury Bakers contribute a sort of tziss, tziss, tziss, like cymbals. Very good for the rhythm section. Then there are the tiny squeaks which come from our littlest relations, the Tom Thumbs. They keep to themselves mostly."

"Are those the names you call each other?"

"Those are the names the Prof gave us. He told us our Latin names too, but we don't like using them. He learned Latin at school and still speaks it occasionally. He's a bit old fashioned in some ways. No, we just call each other by our first names."

"Your songs are very important to you, aren't they?"

"Gwynneth says they are our life. It's how we start new life, she says. I'm not sure how the songs do that. I haven't got to that part yet."

"I'd like to listen to your song some day."

"You may have to stand back a little. I won't give you a blast now. That would definitely wake Ted up. I know he'd really love to eat me, and that could spoil my day completely. I wouldn't want that today because I'm feeling quite excited; I can feel a quest underway. How about I give you a few bars next time I come here? I could sing on approach. Actually, we're not too good in the air, we really need a branch to resonate on. I'll tell you what I'll do, I can manage a sort of distress call on approach, then I'll settle up the tree somewhere and give you my best rendition at full blast. Will you keep an eye out for the birds?"

"I can assure you no birds set wing in this garden. Not even up the top of this tree. Ted was a demon in his younger days. A few Indian Mynas made the mistake of walking up and shouting at him one day, and he was just so fast. I was just a baby, I had to look away. The humans weren't too impressed either with the blood and feathers all over the place. You wouldn't think it to look at him now, poor old Ted. So, will you come tomorrow?"

"Yes. I have nothing on tomorrow. I really hope tonight we can figure out something we small people can do to help."

"You can sing, can't you? Everybody loves a song. Even inanimate objects would like a song. How about a summer song for Sydney... that's got to be a good place to start, sport."

"We *could* sing, couldn't we! Thanks Monty. I'll see you tomorrow. Say goodbye to Ted for me."

As Gerry fluttered his erratic way back through the Park, tracking from tree to tree, aiming for the small dense ones which gave better cover than the huge wide-limbed figs, he wondered why this cat who could eat him in a second was apparently happy and undemanding with his company. Was this a brief indulgence? Was it foreplay to an appetizer? Was there a reason the big black cat would want him as a confidant?

He vowed to keep alert. But it was a chore being wary. Cicadas prefer to be open and straightforward, they are not normally suspicious.

But Gerry was beginning to suspect he wasn't a normal cicada.

Still, he had gathered an awful lot of information for his small brain to carry and as he fluttered he was happy to return to the matter at hand. Or, at claw, as cicadas say.

Did he have some good stuff to deliver to this evening's meeting? Was Monty pointing in the right direction? Could a song make a difference?

Chapter Seven

The room was buzzing. As you would expect with a room full of cicadas. Without an obvious lead from the front the males were very happy to make their own sounds, chirruping gently to keep their vocals warm and comfortable. This gave them a wonderful surge of pleasure as, in any other location outside this room, even a gentle clearing of the drums in preparation for a full blast intended to attract a girlfriend was to put your life on the line. A swoop of sleek feathers, a merciless beak and you were another tiny tragedy, another one of the appalling high numbers of cicadas swept away for the love of a summer song.

The trees of Sydney are full of birds: the huge but slow moving Kookaburras, the largest member of the global kingfisher family, but they are serious meat eaters.

Then the black and white Currawongs with their terrifying golden eyes and the slightly smaller but still substantial Magpies also black and white with coppery eyes were fearsome and fast attackers. Even their children, who grew rapidly to the same size as their parents but dressed in grey and white for their first year, were quick off the mark. They mostly followed their mother, pathetically squeaking to be fed, but the lethal employment of quick eyes and beaks was a skill soon learned.

Cicadas actually have a guarded respect for the Magpies. Although the fearsome flapping approach and swoop might mean death, on a summer evening concealed from sight amongst the leaves the cicadas really appreciated the Magpies' singing in groups in the trees around them.

For cicadas love of song is absolute. They admire and envy the many-noted warble of the Magpies, sometimes solo, often in a tree-filling choir as they produced a sparkling contribution to morning and evening song,

Ironically cicadas most feared the fast-flying Noisy Miners ... home-grown death on grey wings.

All cicadas are scared of them, as the human residents of Sydney are of sharks. But the 'accident' rate is actually very low. The Miners certainly fling themselves ferociously through the branches, however they are not cicada-eaters but honey-eaters. Their preferred food comes from blossoms, flowers and fruits. There is plenty of gossip but no recorded instances of fatal Miner attacks.

Also to be reckoned with, are the unfortunately imported black Indian Mynas. But again they are not confirmed killers. All upstart and cocky they appear to be just as happy walking along the ground searching for scraps as flying for their food.

Cicadas are not born with precise knowledge of their predators but those who survive more than a week build undefined but ominous images in their minds of the different threats, in the way that humans may have several poorly visualised but recurring images in their nightmares.

So when they found themselves free to behave with no inhibitions in this high-up city room, they were grateful to the good old Prof. Only a tiny percentage of privileged Sydney cicadas knew about this place. Those present were all born and bred in nearby city parks on the roots of city trees. Most were from Hyde Park, some from the Domain and a very few from the harbour-fronting Botanic Gardens.

So they hummed happily, with a shriek here and there as one of the younger ones had trouble with their tuning.

Occasionally they would leg it up to a neighbour and exchange greetings through close rubbings, but mostly they were self contained.

The females in the room of course were not singers, but they were good cuddlers, and they teased the boys as they brushed past.

These always silent girls were serene, happy to be close to so many attractive males. But there was absolutely no thought of taking anything further in this room. So controlled were their emotions that an exchange of glances was not even considered.

But back home in the park? Ah, yes something might happen there.

On the side tables were a few young branches of various gum leaves but no one appeared interested in them. All had assembled in the accepted formation for an important meeting. Row upon row upon row, facing forward towards a polished mahogany box, about the size of a shoe box, which had been placed at one end of the oval table. No one could ever remember seeing the box open but Gerry had heard from some of the older cicadas that it contained men.

The only man in the room was Professor Merac, seated quietly to one side chatting to Cir Franklin and

Gerry could not imagine anything more than one of his manly hands fitting in the box, let alone a lot of 'men'. Maybe Merac knew what was really in there. It was not about to be revealed tonight as Cir Franklin finished his conversation and flew heavily across the short distance to the box, landing well enough but still skidding on the polished surface. It was not really necessary to bring the room to order. Everyone knew the drill. The cicadas' inherent politeness and their unceasing sensitivity to every detail around them made them a perfect audience.

But Cir Franklin, as they all knew he would, made a song and dance about taking up his position and delivered a low grumble from his drums. He allowed it to swell briefly to a quaking rumble then cut it short with a deft kick from his back leg. He was a fan of big band music and he'd picked up that move watching a conductor on an old movie he'd seen on TV.

Everybody smiled as usual.

Cir Franklin began.

"Tonight I want to talk to you about a quest. I have been discussing this at some length with our good friend the Professor who I'm pleased to say sees some merit in it. It has been a concern to me that during my presidency, the world has not become a noticeably better place. I still observe friction and frustration and I wonder what we small people can do to help in some small way…"

Gerry chirruped with excitement. In a classroom he would have had his hand up pumping the air, shouting "Ask me sir, ask me!"

Cir Franklin glanced up directly at Gerry but did not respond. Gerry felt a strange connection and saw clearly that the jewels on his leader's head were unusually vibrant. Merac had told Cir to keep his eyes on this young chap.

"From our research, we have found out that the greatest causes of unhappiness in humans are the abrasion of their relationships with each other. Between woman and man, parents and children, workers and bosses, customers and servers, have and have-nots. They have disagreements with neighbours, with complete strangers in crowds, in queues, on the roads. So much for brotherly love. On a large scale this fraternal friction leads to war and famine, on a daily basis it leads to local courts and bloody noses.

Unfortunately we don't think we are big enough to tackle those problems.

We can't do anything there. That's human nature.

However we also know that humans also experience a lot of unhappiness with the 'things' in their lives.

The inanimate objects which get in their way and stubbornly refuse to cooperate; don't behave consistently or predictably. These are generally small things. Which makes it our size of problem. And we believe we have a way of getting to them. Doctor Meracanthus and I believe Inanimate Objects are unhappy because they are ignored and taken for granted, and *that* is why they behave contrarily. If we can talk to them and let them know we understand their plight, perhaps then they will behave better, and then more humans will be happy."

Cir Franklin was quite pleased with the way he summed it all up in that last sentence. He could not resist a satisfying low grumble.

"Doctor Meracanthus will explain more in a moment."

There was a buzz in the room. Most of what had just been said was news to the assembly. The majority had very little contact with humans, let alone discussed their daily troubles with them. The cicadas knew they lived in a city of men. They flew over them daily. They were well aware of the difference between natural and built, trees and houses, earth and concrete. They all knew Merac was a man and knew that they were in his building which was constructed by man. But their day by day lives spun simply around a relationship with the trees of the parks, the sap they contained and the birds they attracted.

But everyone of them was attentive, loyal and faithful ... if our leader says there is something we can do, then by all means let us give it a go.

Merac rose. There was absolutely no irony in his stance or voice as he turned to the three sides of the table acknowledging his audience of several hundred tiny creatures. He had known them or their predecessors all of his professional life and had grown to admire their humble decency. He enjoyed their company.

Deciding to open his talk with a little flourish of entertainment, he knew he was putting the reward before the assignment, but that was OK.

He held up his two open palms facing to his left, the centre and his right. He closed his left hand into a fist and from it with his right fingers pulled a necklace of gum leaves strung together, a couple of metres long. He flicked it like a whip and then threaded it in a crumpled bunch into his right hand. He threw it in the air and it exploded in a pooff of smoke. Gone.

The cicadas loved it. Some of the younger ones let out an uncontrolled chirrup.

Gwynneth glared, as always, but saw that Cir Franklin was beaming, as always.

"Some of you may know..." began Merac, although of course ALL of them knew. They had either seen him in action before or had been told about it and were eagerly awaiting their first performance.

" ... that I like to do magic tricks. I'm not very good ..."

He reached behind his ear and produced a struggling bird with its wings flapping. A Noisy Miner

The fear in the room was immediate. Hundreds of legs scratched backwards. There was even a smattering of wings preparing for reverse take offs.

Merac calmed the bird with his other hand. Calmed it so much it turned into a silk handkerchief which he tucked into his top pocket.

He executed a little bow and smiled at the crowd. He produced some coins from his pocket. The cicadas who had seen them before loved the coin tricks. Merac had to modify these from the ones he did for his more usual human audiences as he could not produce a fifty cent piece from behind a cicada's ear quite as convincingly as he could from behind a child's. But he could make a pile of gum leaves turn into a sparkling stack of twenty cents and he could, taking unfair advantage of a cicada's limited turning capacity, make a spinning five cent appear suddenly behind them.

As he looked up he saw a very lovely woman walk quietly into the room. She closed the door very carefully and held a finger to her lips. She was holding a sleeping child over her shoulder. Merac smiled straight at her. Her presence seemed to inspire him to greater enthusiasm.

"When my grandfather first started teaching me tricks, and I was making plenty of mistakes, he used to quote a man called Adam Hull Shirk, who warned that the art of magic was full of pitfalls, no matter how hard you practice. Mr Shirk said that *'It is an established fact that in nine cases out of ten, whatever can go wrong in a magical performance will do so. The great professors of the art are not immune from the malignancy of matter and the eternal cussedness of inanimate objects'*

That line always stayed with me. Not just because as I practised my magic I was always running up against decks of cards that wouldn't do what my fingers wanted, and coins that clattered on the floor instead of disappearing into thin air, and eggs that produced a bulge clearly visible to the audience instead of hiding in the silk folds as I wanted, but also in all sorts of non-magic objects.

I asked my friends and family and sure enough they felt the same as me. Whether they were playing sport, at work, in the kitchen, doing things round the house, so many of them found themselves saying when something small went wrong: 'How on earth did it do that!' 'It shouldn't do that!' and 'That thing has a mind of its own!'

It was amazing how many said 'It couldn't do that again if it tried!' and 'You couldn't do that in a million years.' If it was just as easy for this 'thing' to do something right, why did it choose to do something wrong?

Here were intelligent, rational people wondering why this 'thing' appeared to be deliberately misbehaving. They'd spend a couple of seconds glaring at the offender and then, being intelligent rational people, realise that there couldn't have been anything deliberate.

But it happens so often.

So I began to wonder if matter is malignant and inanimate objects display their cussedness on a regular basis, maybe they *do* know what they're doing.

But why? Why do they make our lives miserable? What have we done to them?

We ignore them, that's what. We only acknowledge that they are there when we are shouting at them because we think they have let us down.

It is my, *our*, theory that all they need is some recognition. Some acknowledgement that they are there and they are important to us. We can't go on ignoring them..."

Cir Franklin scratched forward on the mahogany box.

"We thought we could offer the inanimate objects a universal signal of recognition, a sign they are not forgotten..."

Merac interrupted

"Have any of you seen a rainbow? All those colours? You'd know if you'd seen one..."

Quite a few of the assembly raised a wing.

"There is a saying amongst humans that the first rainbow appeared after a great flood. The rain lasted 40 days and 40 nights..."

Cicadas don't mind some gentle rain but that sounded like way too much and there was a scattered gasp of displeasure.

"...and when it ended God made a covenant with man, he promised such a flood wouldn't happen again and as a sign of good faith he showed man the rainbow. Today a lot of people look at a rainbow and believe it is a sign that they are not forgotten and are still appreciated. We can't drum up a rainbow but we can give the inanimate objects something else. When they hear it they know they are appreciated by us and they have not been forgotten."

Cir Franklin took over again.

"What we cicadas have always had, and what we are very good at, is a song. Of course it must be a special song. Not just our regular one. A special note. We have heard there is a magical note with such power. Merac says it can break things, it has the power to shatter a wineglass. Now that is a powerful note! That's the one we need to demonstrate that we have the power."

Gerry had a fleeting thought that at least one inanimate object might not reckon this was such a great idea and that was a wine glass. He looked across at Merac who seemed to read his mind and nodded, but held his finger to his lips as a sign they could address that little problem a little later.

"All we have to do is find this note. " Cir Franklin paused for effect. The room was suitably hushed. "When we sung the word around we were given a clue that the name of the person who can produce this note most perfectly is engraved on a bronze tablet not all that far from here. If ... when, we have that name, we are well on the way to Mastering the Note and Perfecting the Song. We can then tune our songs, and pass the word on to the Inanimate Objects that that is Their Song. When they hear that note they will know they are not forgotten.

They will all be so grateful to be recognised and they will become less grumpy, less dogged and become more willing and more co-operative with humans.

If it works then our work will be done. A small gesture but an important one in a world where every little helps."

He saw Gwynneth looking at him with what he took to be admiration. He certainly had the gift of the gab tonight he thought. He was riding high. He crawled slowly to the front of the box. He made a point of slowly swivelling left then right. His eloquence took on borrowed wings.

"We need someone to undertake the quest. It will not be easy. It involves one of you going boldly where no cicada has ever gone before. A leap into the unknown. It will entail a flight longer than any cicada has ever done. There will be danger. We do not know what is on the other side. The mission is not just there, but there and back. But the rewards are immeasurable. Just one of you will do this for us all. Ask not what this gathering can do for you, but what you can do for this gathering…"

He swung from side to side, overreaching with excitement; "We will fight them on the beaches! Once more into the breach! I have a dream!"

He caught Gwynneth's eyes. That was not admiration. He cleared his drums and brought his speech to an end closing with the words: "I'm calling it my 'Jewelled Vision Quest."

Merac wanted to put in a final word, a genuine statement of his respect for the good creatures who faced him: "I know one of you can do this, I believe in you. I ask you to believe in yourselves. You are better than you think. You will find a way."

Before he could sit down a Cherrynose up the back fluttered to indicate that he wanted to comment. Cir Franklin acknowledged him. Again. There is always someone in every classroom can be relied on to drop in the awkward remark or question. Sometimes it means they have not been paying attention. Sometimes it means they had been paying too much attention, and possibly spotted and inconsistency or weakness in the presentation offered. Little Charly fitted in the second category. He had a knack of coming up with the question that re-opened debate when all seemed settled.

"Cir. How will we know if these inanimate objects have heard us and understood? How will they get back to us with their appreciation?"

Cir deferred to Merac who was still on his feet.

"It would obviously be nice if you could see an immediate change in their performance. But as they *are* inanimate and as their cussedness is often irregular and infrequent that may be difficult. This will be a slow process. But our theory is that if you make an impression on them you should be able to feel it. Probably in the same way as you feel emotions between yourselves. You should feel some kind of awareness in your ocelli ..." Merac indicated by tapping his fingers to his forehead " ... a sort of glow of recognition in your jewels ..."

Seizing his moment, Cir Franklin rose up, his heavy body hovering, the whirring of his wings the only sound in the room until his booming voice took over "Which is why I am calling it my Jewelled Vision Quest."

He said it in such a firm manner, his eyes fixed steadily on Little Charly, that he clearly meant QED ... that's it, that's all folks ... and thereby signalled the winding up of the formal part of the proceedings.

As the crowd buzzed and chirped, breaking their formal formation into small chatting groups, Merac went to the back of the room. He kissed his sleeping daughter and then his wife. She handed their child over and he held the small warm body against him.

"How has she been?"

"Just the same."

"One day..."

"I know. One day." She put her hand on his shoulder. "That part of your speech about Adam Hull Shirk, which you always use..."

"Yes"

"I found out some more about him. He was a scriptwriter in Hollywood in the 1920s."

"Really, I just knew his magic and his quotes. You know that bit where he says : '*whatever can go wrong ... will do so ...*'? I was just thinking as I said it *that* time that it sounds..."

"Sounds like the beginning of Murphy's Law."

"You're right."

"But wait. I have something more for you. I did some research."

She unwrapped a piece of paper from her bag and read from her own writing.

"*It is an experience common to all men, that, on any special occasion, such as the production of a magical effect for the first time in public, everything that can go wrong, will go wrong. Whether we must attribute this to the malignity of matter or to the total depravity of inanimate things, whether the exciting cause is hurry, worry or what not, the fact remains.*"

"Hang on a sec, who said that?"

"A British stage magician by the name of Nevil Maskelyne."

"When?"

"Nineteen hundred and eight."

"Wow. Almost the same words. Is that just great magical minds thinking alike? Or a bit of collusion behind the illusion? If I may say, as a famous magician myself, I can tell you both those gentlemen were spot on about the *depravity* or *cussedness* of inanimate objects. There's two more great minds agreeing that inanimate objects are just pretending to be inanimate. The little buggers know what they're up to all the time."

"You've always said that."

"I remember my Grandad, the first time he let me have his little bean bags to juggle, he told me to throw them on the floor one at a time. Then pick them up and start practising. And every single day when you practice, throw them on the floor one at a time before you start. He said that's where they'll keep heading, that's where they'll end up sooner or later, so you knock some of the stubbornness out of them by throwing them on the floor. All inanimate objects have a pact with gravity, he said, and you never take gravity lightly."

"Good advice."

"So the world thinks Murphy's Law came from Edwards Airforce Base in the sixties but Adam Hull Shirk, Nevil Maskelyne, the two of us and now the cicadas think different."

"Looks that way. Are you going to choose Gerry for the Quest? Adam Hull Shirk would be glad too."

"I'm sure he would; he knew a lot about inanimate objects."

"He also wrote the script for a movie in 1924 called *'Leave it to Gerry'*"

Chapter Eight

Inanimate objects don't have meetings.

They simply can't get there.

Unless a human moves them around they tend to just hang around with other objects in the vicinity.

Many stay still forever.

Some are products of nature, like rocks, others are man-made like houses. Man gives 'birth' to them but doesn't give life to them.

The world is full of inanimate things. The very rock we stand on for a start. There are several levels of inanimacy. Major species of inanimates include planets. Minor ones include specks of dust.

But in the middle are the ones that are of most concern to humans. The things around the average household.

Being closer to humans these objects have had time to observe, and some of them slowly but surely develop awareness and even feelings. In some cases their dispositions become settled and benign, possibly even contented. For some it is a pleasure just to sit there, say nothing and watch the world go by. A stone wall fits this description. Others find themselves being busy all the time, whether they like it or not.

A teaspoon for example.

Objects particularly hate being used as tools, although some of them have pride in a job well done when they are in the hands of good craftsmen. Being a tool often means a violent and noisy life involving major concussions which wear you down until you are thrown away and spend the rest of your life in some smelly landfill.

On the other hand, some Inanimate Objects have a very happy life. Especially if you are in close contact with a human who actually likes you, perhaps even loves you and begins to share confidences with you.

A bracelet for example. Most pieces of jewellery are in this category. Pens and watches. Some items of clothing.

Happy little pieces indeed. You never hear a peep out of them.

But then there are the many many others who are grumpy and resentful. Tired of being taken for granted. Sick of the lack of recognition. Outraged that people refuse to believe they may have feelings too.

These are the ones that give you grief.

These are the ones that drop, slip, fall, spill, snag, hide, scratch, crack and even break.

These are the ones you shout at or hit when they fail to act immediately as you want.

Staring angrily at the useless object you find yourself wondering is this simple incompetence on its part, or active defiance...

You must believe now that this cussedness is real. It will be ongoing and it is not going to get better if we keep our heads in the sand.

It's time we did something about it.

Chapter Nine

A flutter of leaves can be exhilarating for a cicada.

High winds are a consideration for any winged creature from a jumbo jet to a bee,

and cicadas find a really strong blow flings them around as they come in to a tree.

However a gentle breeze in the right kind of leaves can present as much fun and challenge to a landing cicada as a surfer catching a wave on an unfamiliar beach. Sometimes they'll grab the nearest moving leaf and work their way down to a safe branch from there. Gerry, always the adventurer even in small things, usually tried to thread through the outer flurry of foliage and hit a branch first time. Sometimes it worked. Other times he was able to practice his 'uh oh' recovery manoeuvres.

Trees are just trees to most humans. Yes, they know big from small. Most can tell a local gum tree or eucalyptus from an import, such as a fir or pine. But they don't depend on them for dear life as cicadas do. A sound knowledge of trees is a requisite for the little creatures.

Late the next afternoon, Gerry was descending one of the great Port Jackson figs, the majestic guardians filling the air around Hyde Park. Their leaves, small for such giants, massed like low clouds above the stone flagged walkways leading to the inner city squares of grass. They were as huge and old as Gerry was young and green.

He reversed down one of the natural furrows, moving very slowly in its purple shadows, his skinny legs like scratchy pistons, pumping silently. He hoped his stealth would render his dramatic greenness less conspicuous against the smooth grey bark.

The low sun tingled on his jewels. Gerry was on a mission and all his body felt lit and ready.

The park wasn't very crowded. The centre of Sydney does thin out a bit after working hours. Many city workers go home to their houses in the suburbs. The family friendly bungalow with pool on a quarter acre block was long the preferred home of the Sydneysider and spread of this kind of dwelling has pushed the boundaries of Greater Sydney 50 kilometres in each direction. Except East, where the ocean is. Unlike New York's much larger Central Park there are few high rise apartment blocks surrounding

Hyde Park. Mainly shops, office buildings, churches and schools.

Hyde Park may be full on a sunny lunch hour, or when it is hosting an event or festival, but even on a splendid summer evening like this, passersby were few.

That's OK by me, Gerry noted, looking for his first Great Experiment.

Swivelling around on a small branch about three metres above ground level his first thought was there is a scarcity of inanimate objects around here. Well, ones that are within his size range. He could see buildings, the fountain. Some statues. Rubbish bins. Pathways. Is a path an Inanimate Object? Hmmm, sort of. It is certainly inanimate, but it is continuous. Linked to miles of other pathways. Hardly an 'object'. Gerry thought an object should have finite edges, and those not too far apart from each other. He would define one as something a human could pick up.

A girl with a dog bounced past. Her dress swished quite animatedly. Her bag was inanimate but didn't seem to be doing anything wrong. The dog had a soggy tennis ball in its mouth. But it was carried away before Gerry could really check it out. He concluded it wasn't doing anything wrong either.

To his left he watched a man walking towards him eating a meat pie. The last piece was protruding from a paper bag, and he finished it off with a couple of quick bites.

He wiped his lips on the bag and crumpled it into a ball. In the same movement he flicked it at the bin he was passing. Neatly done, thought Gerry. The man had sized up and timed his last bite precisely for that bin.

Unfortunately the shot was not so precise.

The paper ball danced off the rim of the bin and bounced onto the path.

Gerry held his breath.

All cicadas are very clean and tidy creatures. Their footprint on the earth is tiny but it is always neat. They abhor rubbish.

The man stopped and turned. He was going to Do the Right Thing. Could he be a conscientious observer of the Keep Australia Beautiful campaign? Or a sportsman miffed at the incomplete shot?

His second shot was upwind but Gerry, a fine judge of wind and angles, thought he had given it just enough and allowed nicely for the conditions. The paper ball hovered dead centre then dropped onto the base of an upturned plastic bottle wedged into the bin. It seemed to find some springiness there and leapt once more over the side.

 You couldn't do that in a million years, thought Gerry.

The man thought so too.

His picked up the paper ball again, said something intimidating to it and scrunched it firmly in his fist. He threw it straight down into the bin. With force.

Defiantly it bounced out! Paper doesn't bounce.

Gerry knew cussedness when he saw it.

The movement of some leaves above him allowed some rays of sun to touch his branch. He settled his legs and wings and gave his drums their voice. Maybe it's a long shot. But it's worth a try.

The man heard the first scratchy warbles. Not the prettiest noise but the true sound of Sydney summer evening. The song although solo swelled into a decent screech. Maybe a good sign for the next couple of days, thought the man. It would be great if we had a good beach weekend.

Again he took up the paper ball, addressed it one more time and held it in two fingers just above the centre of the bin. He dropped it.

As he would tell his mates in the pub later that evening, he could not believe what he saw.

The freed ball took off at an angle as though it had its own mind.

"I'm not kidding. It struck the inside of the rim and travelled at least half way round it, like that putt I did on the ninth last week. Half way round it bounced down onto something in the bin, then out onto the rim again and kept going. Musta been a coupla seconds. It was like it was alive!"

The paper ball, after its extraordinary display, behaving as if at the whim of an unknown animator, settled comfortably in the bin like any other piece of rubbish.

The man shook his head and moved on, glancing in the direction of the unseen but clearly heard cicada.

Gerry was thrilled.

This is really working.

Was it the song or was it the wind? Gerry chose to believe in the song.

Chapter Ten

"You beauty, that's a piece of bloody good news. Mind you it was coming my way. I've earned it, mate."

Harold hung up the phone.

"What's that, sir?" Paul enquired.

"We'll get the go ahead on that big new job on Bennelong Point."

"There's an Opera House already there, sir."

"Don't be a smart arse. The next stage. No one else will get a look in, because no one else will be told about it. If they're forced to tender, we'll still be right. Get us a drink will you."

"What stage is this? Are they really serious about the apartments in the Gardens?"

"Nope, that's some way off. We'll keep those plans on ice. You never know. Maybe a change of government's needed there..."

Harold's mind drifted to pleasant thoughts.

"We'll blow the bastard up. That's what we'll do."

"The Opera House."

"Nah, what do you think I am. That's an icon. Can't touch that. At least not this time around. The car park's all we get."

"There's a perfectly good car park already there."

"There's going to be a much bloody bigger one."

Paul opened a bottle of the John Riddoch. The deep crimson gurgled into the biggest of their Riedel glasses.

"They've been wanting a better carpark there for years. No one's ever been happy with the one they've got. They were too wimpy when the built the first one. All the preservation nonsense, the conservation of that cliff under Government House. If they'd knocked the cliff down, no one would miss it and you could have a really nice building instead of that grubby rock face.

"The Tarpeian Way."

"The what?"

"That's what they call that cliff. Named after some Roman site where they threw people to their death." "Jesus, Paul where do you come up with this stuff? No one's been thrown off there. Have they? Woulda been in the papers."

"I think it may be an ironic name, sir."

"Spare me your irony."

"What building have you in mind?"

"A big one, a beaut new carpark to match the Opera House. Cover it with white tiles. Maybe we can have big white sails. Maybe Roman arches. The architects'll sort that stuff out. Maybe have a restaurant or a club in there as well. Easy. But expensive. And we get the gig. Just need the old carpark to become suddenly obsolete. You know, unstable, unusable, unparkable..."

Paul nodded. Waiting for the summation.

"Explosives do that."

Paul took a sip of his wine.

"Know anyone?" said Harold.

"Anyone what?"

"Anyone good with explosives."

"Sir!"

"Serious, Paul. Ask around."

Chapter Eleven

"It's a long way for a little fella, Gerry."

"I'll be alright."

Gerry was crawling across a map of Sydney Harbour that Merac had spread on the boardroom table. Beside them was the chess board laid out. These were the 'men' that were in the mahogany box. A fine weighted Staunton tournament set by Jacques and Son of London. It had belonged to Merac's grandfather. Merac was teaching Gerry to play. He had to shift the pieces for him as Gerry crawled between the towering black and white figures to indicate his preferred piece and its move.

Merac tapped the map.

"There's the Pool there."

"I see it." said Gerry.

"If your eyesight was good enough..."

"Nothing wrong with my eyes."

"... or if you had a telescope," Merac continued, "you could see it from where you were born. There is a direct line of sight from the Opera House past Admiralty House."

"It doesn't show my trees on this map."

"No, but you know where they are."

Gerry crawled over to the spot where, although unmarked on this map, two forest red gums stood on the cliff just above the Opera House. Twin Reds. The forest red gum could be one of the largest of the urban eucalypts. It would be a king if it grew freely, away from the city, hundreds of kilometres west on the banks of one of the inland rivers.

"How long since you've been there?" Merac asked gently.

"Years."

Merac smiled. He loved this little man. Bold, optimistic. He was much more than a glass-half-full person. If you could put sap in a glass, Gerry's would be always brimming.

"Well, some time ago." Gerry revised his guess.

"Probably last week." Merac suggested.

"Maybe you're right. I buzz up to the park most days, call in on Monty, and I've been in here the last couple of days ... haven't I?"

"Yes you have."

"Why do you think Cir Franklin picked me?"

"I told him you were an exceptionally good flyer. We know this trip is probably further than any cicada has ever flown. If you think about it most of your flights take only seconds. For this you will be going over water for up to five or six minutes."

"I fly down to see Monty. That takes a good couple of minutes"

"I know, that's what I told Cir Franklin. I also said you were brave and resourceful, and I thought you had the intelligence to make the right decisions along the way. I told him about your conversations with Monty. I told him you had already proved our theory with your triumph of the paper ball in the park bin."

"You're right. We're half way there aren't we?"

"We have a long way to go Gerry."

Chapter Twelve

"Good morning, Mr... er...."

"Call me Guy. Everyone does."

Paul attempted to shake hands but was offered a cross-handed left fist expertly reversed for shaking. He noticed there were only three fingers on it.

Through the gloom he could see the right hand resting on the timber edge of bar top had a glossy painted look to it.

Paul felt more than uneasy. But this was what the Boss wanted. He had directed him to this old pub in The Rocks with a name to ask for. "Had to do your bloody homework for you!"

Paul doubted the Boss had ever been here although you never knew with Harold. It didn't look like the sort of venue that would serve John Riddoch by the glass. Or even have wine glasses.

Paul looked Guy in the eye. Not quite. The eye he could see wandered off to the side then flicked back. The other eye, if it was in fact still there, was behind a black leather patch held by a leather strap across a forehead lined with age and ancient scars.

"Can I buy you a drink? "

"Reschs"

Paul beckoned to the barmaid. He had asked her when he came in if she knew a Reginald Forks. Without emotion she had nodded in the direction of this not quite complete human being with the crutches leaning on the bar beside his stool. As his eyes adjusted to the change of light from the shimmering summer day outside, he could see no-one else in the low light of the small sandstone-walled room. The girl followed him down on her side of the bar.

He ordered two middies.

The barmaid raised a painted brow and went off smiling. She set the two beers down. Foam slithered down the sides. Paul would not normally be drinking beer at midday but a mission is a mission. He watched as Guy's three fingered hand, two fingers and a thumb actually, reached for his beer. The curving digits didn't quite close around their quarry. Nonetheless he lifted his arm and the hand rose clear of the glass. He repeated the move again and again, seeming to try harder each time, but not succeeding. Each time the fingers failed to grip and the glass remained on the bar.

Guy turned his face to Paul's and said with a surprisingly sweet smile:

"Hand only fits schooners."

Paul then noticed that the empty glass Guy had recently finished was a larger size.

He didn't have to beckon the barmaid. She hadn't left.

"Schooners?" she said.

"Schooners." said Paul.

"Pull up a pew." said Guy moving his crutches to his other side, keeping his back to the wall at the end of the bar.

Paul noticed his companion's trouser leg was folded and pinned up. He hadn't seen that since photos of his grandfather after he came back from the war having lost a leg.

He took a sip from his new larger beer.

"I was told to ask you about, er ...explosives."

"You've come to the right place. Nothing I don't know. Who do you want killed?"

"No-one. No-one."

"What do youse want explosives for? You know they hurt people."

"Is that what, er … hurt you? Your hand, er … hands?""

"Early days."

"Your eye? Same early days?"

"Nah, those were different early days."

Paul noticed a large, old fashioned hearing aid when Guy brushed back his lengthy hair.

"Your leg?"

"Another early day."

"Your ear?"

'Yeah, that was fairly early days. But, I kept at it. I'd made up me mind to be good at it."

"So no recent losses?"

"Nup. But then there's not been a lot of work around."

"But you keep your hand in?"

"In a manner of speaking." Guy waved his right hand.

"Have you done any big jobs?"

"In the bush I have. Done a lot of blasting for the open-cut mines. I can bring down half a mile of cliff face."

"So fifty metres would be easy?"

"Piece of cake."

Paul pulled a panoramic photo from his coat pocket. He brushed his index finger across the surface.

"Could you bring down this cliff face and um, destroy that entrance there?"

"I've seen that place. Where is it again?"

"How far back could you take that cliff?"

"As far as you like. Just depends on the charges and how much drilling we can do."

"I don't think we'll have the opportunity for drilling."

"Just surface? Weeelll … we can make a bit of a mess."

"A bit of a mess might do it."

Guy starred at the photo bending his head forward creakily until it brushed Paul's sleeve.

"Ah, I can see it now. Are you seriously gunna blow up the Opera House?"

"Not the Opera House per se. The carpark, which is some way away."

"You'd bring down half the bloody windows in Macquarie Street! Probably kill some poor bastards as well."

"We're hoping not. It's all a matter of timing."

"You telling me it is!" Guy studied his good hand.

"Can you do it?"

"Anything's possible. Might cost a bit."

"There will be no problem with money."

"For my stuff or for me?"

"Both."

"I got a stash on a mate's property outside Gosford. A few boxes of old mining stuff I pinched before they pissed me off. Quite a pile there, now I think of it. Might be a bit unstable, but this could be a good way to get rid of the lot."

"Instability is not a word we like. We'd rather pay good money for a good job."

"Yeah, I'm with ya. But people tend to notice when blokes like me try to buy Semtex and C4. Though I reckon I can get some through a mate. It'll cost ya."

"You can do the job?"

"Big job, isn't it? Important to you. Well important to who you're working for. It'll make a bloody mess for a while. Is that what you want? There's going to be a helluva stink, you know that. They'll be looking for the blokes what done it. I'd need to be far away when it happens."

"Perhaps you could arrange to 'disappear' in the explosion." Paul winked "Then they wouldn't come looking for you."

"That's a thought. A lot of people would expect me to mess up like that. I don't get a lot of respect anymore. I'll think about that."

"Have you thought about how you might do it?"

"You only just bloody told me about it! But it's pretty straightforward if all you wanna do is bring down a whole lotta rock."

"Well yes that's more or less it."

"Course I have to have a good look at the joint. As it happens that might not be too hard. A mate of mine works there."

"Where?"

"At the car park. He runs it."

"Do we need to involve him?"

"I can't do this on my own, mate. Too much lifting. I'm gunna need a lot of help just to carry stuff. But checking it out, that's the clever bit. As it happens he can probably arrange to put me on as a casual for a couple of days so I can move around the joint. The simplest set up I can manage, to cause the sort of shitfight you're expecting will take me a couple of days.

I'll need a van or ute to come and go a few times. Fair amount of stuff involved, as you can imagine, even if you've never put one of these events together yourself."

"Can we trust your mate?"

"He does have a bit of a dark history. It's not as if the cops are checking on him every day, but he's done his share of time. He knows how this kind of thing works so I reckon he'll be on our side. Also he's been looking for a way out of Sydney for a long while. I'm assuming you can stump up sufficient cash to double the size of your workforce. Me and him. Not as if you'll be paying payroll tax. You want to get things done properly?"

"Well, yes."

"Most importantly for us all he owes me one. Big time."

"I'll have to meet him."

'You OK to move to another boozer? He won't come here. Barred. He'll cost you quite a few schooners. He drinks a bit."

Paul took another sip of his beer. He swallowed, and took another sip. He was falling behind again.

"Perhaps not today ..."

"Nah. Didn't mean today. I'll have a word to him and give you a call."

"How about you have a word and I call you this time tomorrow."

"OK. Play it your way."

"You think this can be done?"

"Mate, I haven't done anything quite like it, obviously. But I can tell you I've done much bigger bangs than you're talking about here. We just have to be a bit careful laying things out. This area is a bit precious to Sydney, so the authorities tend to keep an eye out. The bang's the easy bit. What you are paying for is some supplies, the expertise to wire them up to do the job, but you're also securing the services of a couple of blokes with rat cunning ... with the smarts to stay one jump ahead of the rozzers, and leave the scene with no paw prints. That right?"

'That sounds ... right."

Guy finished his beer. The barmaid took a fresh schooner glass from the fridge and moved to her taps. She didn't even deign to fetch one for the Pommy bloke who was still only half way down his schooner.

Paul slipped another note across the mat.

"Thanks, love" said Guy, musing half to himself. "All electronics now, you see. You save on fuses and matches, even rolls of wire, but they're costly all those other gadgets you need. Timers, detonators, relays. We'll probably use a mobile phone to set it off ...that way you can pick your moment but keep yourself out of sight. I might put the transmitter in a Reschs longneck just for Barry. That would be a nice touch. Baz would get a laugh out of that. We can pack the explosive into witches hats with the detonators. Put 'em in a row round the cliff. People never touch witches hats, they just walk around them. Try it yourself, knock off one from a council and stick it on the footpath. It'll stay there for weeks. Except the kids might kick it ..."

"I have to be going. I'll call this time tomorrow." Paul managed to drain his beer but saw the barmaid going for the fridge. He couldn't take another one.

Outside he took out his mobile and reported back to Harold.

"We're on."

Chapter Thirteen

Gerry had a good meal in the boardroom the night before his Quest began. Lemon scented gum leaves. Yum. Naturally he had chosen his favourite from all of the soft branches arrayed on the long table.

A little earlier, George who was a bit of a Sap Snob had been presiding over a Tasting.

Gerry had arrived just as the group was finishing their deliberations. After so much concentration and discussion, sucking and spitting, they always topped themselves up on the sap they most liked during the tasting. Gwyneth had once described such excessive behaviour as 'twig-swigging.'

Not wishing to interrupt he crawled across to Merac who sat right down the end of the table in his white coat taking notes. While the twelve cicadas were concentrating mainly on aroma and flavour, and discussing those attributes with some fervour, Merac was very keen to cross reference their comments with what he knew about each tree. In his laboratory he had tested most of the species of eucalypt from around Sydney. He knew their genetic makeup, and perhaps more importantly their nutrient value: the sugar levels, vitamins and proteins which the cicadas depended on.

As the comments flew around the table, often followed by the commenter himself, seeking to make a point on another sappy comparison, Merac noted, as he had on many such tastings, which species preferred which sap. And from subsequent interviews he was able to cross reference that information with details of each cicada's age, daily flying distances and energy levels.

Gerry sat quietly beside the notepad watching his fellows carrying on. Gerry did enjoy a fine sap from time to time but he did think these blokes went on a bit.

George was shouting at an elderly Black Prince who had the temerity to praise "some touches of peppermint, delicate citrussy notes and a lingering finish" he'd detected in a twig of Casuarina.

"It's not even a eucalypt, Brendan! You can't make good sap from a *casuarinaceae*!"

"I beg to differ" said Brendan "I have, I believe, tasted more extensively than you George and I find most eucalypts flabby and coarse, some are even woody.

An inrush of breath from those around the table.

Brendan continued in his light and elegant voice. "I give you that Australia's greatest sap, perhaps our only First Growth, the fabulous Branch 95, does come from eucalypt, but there are many other trees that offer a breadth of exceptional flavours."

"Have a suck of this Brendan" George beckoned him over to the piece of red flowering gum he was sitting on.

As Brendan slid his needle-like rostrum into the sweetest slender twig, George couldn't stop himself describing it.

"Note the bouquet - floral, heady, a whiff of red berries, the ..."

"Not from around here, is it?" mumbled the Black Prince, head down.

"Very good, Brendan. The *ficofolia* is originally from West Australia. On the mid-palate you should be getting rich ripe fruit, nuances of plummy jamminess; it's full-bodied with a vibrant, tube-filling presence underpinned by fine supple and elegant notes, finishing with a dash of firming unctuousness ..."

"Rubbish, George, it's a good drinking quaffer. No more."

Gerry could feel Merac's suppressed laughter as he tried to write.

George took it with a laugh himself. Cicadas could never be really angry. In these sessions George often evoked the famous Len Evan's Theory of Consumption and on that they did agree. It stated that life is too short not to drink fine sap every day. Every suck of an inferior branch was like throwing a good one away.

When they silently lurched with full bellies away from their chosen twigs, their tiny legs appearing unsteady, Merac had the thought which had occurred to him before at these tastings. Does the sugar in the sap begin fermenting once the branch is off the tree?

Could these little fellas be getting more than they bargained for? They certainly seemed more vocal at the end of a session. Especially George, who seemed to 'taste' the most.

Merac resolved to take a few branches back to the lab and test them for alcohol.

He turned to Gerry.

"You think this is all nonsense don't you? This tasting and discussion?"

"It's not something I'd get involved in myself. I mean I do like some sap better than others but it's silly to talk about it for hours."

"You didn't tell them that just then. You could've had a go at them. You actually complemented them on their efforts."

"They're my friends."

"So..."

"Can't be anything wrong in making your friends feel good."

Merac left it there. He'd had long conversations with Sondrine about white lies, but Gerry's guileless transparency always floored him. A short life, but a simple and clear one.

Not long after the 'tasters' had left Cir Franklin had flown in.

"Well Gerry. Not long now. Feeling good?"

Gerry was filling up on lemon scented sap. Of course he felt good.

Thinking of the task ahead Merac was quite happy with Gerry's choice. He knew it offered one of the highest levels of nourishment for *cyclochila australasiae* - Gerry's species.

Gerry was allowed to take his time. Cir Franklin and Merac watched over him. Gerry had glanced up in between sucks of the sweet citrussy juice directly into Cir's eyes. They shone shiny and golden brown. The diamonds on his head glittered. Gerry took another suck then slowly shifted his body to look into Merac's eyes. Curiously he found more life there. More compassion? Understanding?

Chapter Fourteen

The flight began with a hiccup.

More of a burp, actually.

Merac met Gerry at the Red Twins just before dawn.

He found him easily because he was quite close to the ground. And had dirt on his claws and wings.

"You OK, Gerry? What are you doing down here?"

"I might be a bit overweight for takeoff. Sucked a lot more than I should. I was a bit emotional last night when I came back here and I thought I'd like a final taste of my

birth sap ... in case anything happened to me."

"Nothing will happen, my friend. You'll sail through."

"Anyway I flew in up the top there and although I'd just had a full sip with you and Cir Franklin I still had a kind of hunger. Then I remembered something someone said at the tasting session about nothing is quite as sweet as the sap you have when you are a baby. The sap you take from the tree roots as a nymph. I can't remember that far back, but I thought I'd give it a go. I worked out where the big roots were from the base of the tree and started to dig. The ground is very hard."

"We haven't had rain for a while. But you have good strong legs. They are designed for digging. Well, for digging *up* when you first come up."

"It's no fun going down I can tell you..."

"Of course you are still protected in your shell when you first emerge."

"I managed to get down to one of the main roots. I was covered in dirt, I could hardly see, but I blew the old rostrum clear of dust and stuck it really deep into the root. A bit tougher than the twigs you serve but well worth the effort. It was magic. It took me right back. No sooner had the cool sap touched my palate than a shudder ran through me. An exquisite pleasure invaded my senses. Where did it come from? What did it mean? I felt like I could go on forever."

"You can Gerry. The brevity of life is illusory."

He picked the little chap up.

"Can you blow that dirt off me. Thanks. I am now ready."

"From here?" Merac held up his opened palm as Gerry wiggled his body to face the Harbour, now glistening pink as it was brushed by the rising sun beyond the huge white sails.

"Where better?"

"Travel well, my little friend. Keep Singing."

Chapter Fifteen

Merac returned to his laboratory. He carried in his inner eyes his last view of Gerry, the vision of that tiny brave creature with his conscientious wings a blurring grey mist around his fully-fuelled body, darting erratically past the sails of the Opera House. To Merac he appeared blindingly and dangerously visible.

He had stared until he lost sight of him against the sunrise.

He was sadder than he had ever felt.

Over his computer, with his key notebook beside him (he always worked with an artist's pad and a 2B propelling pencil with a rubber on the end; in his work he knew that a slick drawing was often worth more than a thousand typed words) he revisited his achingly sad conclusions.

He knew that cicadas, as individuals, have never had long to live.

But he also knew that over recent years he had heard fewer and fewer cicadas in the suburbs even in the heat of summer.

They were suffering the same problems as the big species most people regarded as more important. Reduction of habitat, increase in predators. In the case of cicadas, yes there was a loss of big trees in many established suburbs. Worse, the spread of housing was chewing up whole swathes of bushland. He would admit these were minor compared to the forests of Tasmania, Brazil, Rwanda and Borneo with their donation-worthy creatures - Devils, Jaguars, Gorillas and Orangutans, but still these were fine and lively areas with many small species unable to fend for themselves. The inner city problem was the hard surfacing of areas near trees that had previously been soft and natural waiting to receive the hatched nymphs as they dropped to the ground to burrow in for their seven dark years underground. Merac had also noticed a change in the city's birdlife. Where once he had seen the smaller species of birds, not that much bigger than the largest Floury Baker, such as Robin Red Breasts, Willie Wagtails, Sparrows, Blue Wrens and Peewees thriving in the untouched shrubby patches of bushland still dotting some suburbs, now he only saw the much larger Currawongs and Magpies and plenty of the smaller but unstoppable Noisy Miners.

The city cicadas had a real battle on their hands.

He smiled, remembering that Gerry would certainly have corrected him to say claws.

Ah Gerry. You and your friends who fill these rooms with your simple decency. And all the cicadas who come out new every year. What will happen to you all?

He realised he had drawn three jewels at the points of a triangle. With neat little lines radiating out he made them glow.

Could he do something for these little people?

Chapter Sixteen

"Oh that's awful! Oh no, that's so sad. Oh darling ...."

Merac was driving when his wife sat forward so abruptly her seatbelt creaked. Startled, he was about to hit the brakes, looking to see what she had seen. A child on the road? An animal? The road seemed clear. Something on the footpath?

She had her hand over her mouth and in his periphery he could see she was already beginning the inrushing shrug that signalled she was going to cry.

He saw she was focussed on a car in the lane alongside them, one they had just rolled past as the traffic slowed, an older Renault station wagon in a singular mauve colour. The woman driving was in her thirties with shortish red hair. She was quite clearly sobbing, her shoulders hunching, her hands gripping the wheel. When she realised she was being watched she took one hand off the wheel and wiped her eye. Then changed hands and wiped the other.

She held her head back and swallowed deeply. "It's that song." said Sondrine flicking her hand at the radio in front of her, barely in control of her own voice.

The radio tuned to a classic FM rock station was playing so softly that Merac scarcely registered the melody and voice, but clearly Sondrine had.

Eric Clapton was singing:

"Would you hold my hand, if I saw you in heaven,
Would you help me stand..."

Both lanes had stopped. With their car a length ahead they did not look round. Merac turned to his stricken wife who took his hand on the wheel, rubbing at her cheek with the other.

"I know that girl. I know she's listening to that song. Oh my God, her boy must have died..."

"What are you talking about?"

"I used to see that girl at the hospital a year or so ago. I remember her car and, well ... I remember her. Her boy .... oh God ... It's that song isn't it? We talked about cars and radios. Her car was like a tip. Full of all sorts of rubbish, hers and her boys. She said she never changed the radio. She had it serviced once and they left it on that station so she kept it there. She must be listening to that song now. Oh, I feel for her..."

"Do you want to stop? Maybe talk to her?"

"No no, Please just keep driving."

They drove on, both listening to the radio until it faded across to something a lot livelier from the Rolling Stones.

When they arrived at the hospital, it seemed again to Sondrine as though it was humming with its own life, almost sobbing with its gentle thrum of electronic assistance.

This was a children's hospital and the walls were decorated with bright primaries and patterns, vivacious artworks and sculptures, colourful distractions for the littlies.

Passing some rooms you could not help but hear an occasional cry. Brave kids, very few of them there for the first time, the lovely curves and dimples of the skin nature gave them crossed by tape and tubes.

A place of unimaginable sadness, but each day there was cheerfulness and resolve. The eyes of those in charge remained dry and bright.

Merac parked and met Sondrine near the entrance. They held hands as they walked the familiar corridors.

They found Pix in her room. Assisted in her sleep, she appeared so small in the bed; he anticipated his wife's inrush of breath and her squeeze of his hand.

They had sat with the sounds so many times the beeps now seemed to be her own.

"Shall I get the nurse? They said the doctor had been earlier today."

"I'd like to talk to the doctor. We have time."

Merac went out and returned. They waited.

The doctor who Merac had known from university rugby days opened his hands: "Merac, I'm sorry we just don't know. She just sleeps."

The nurse smiled broadly "We call her Sleeping Beauty."

"All that equipment, the respirator, the tubes, she doesn't seem to need. We've taken her off for hours at a time, kept watch on the monitors and there is no measurable difference in any of her vitals. It's deep sleep with no anticipation of wakefulness. We need that tube to feed her of course. As far as we can tell she is taking everything beautifully. Even growing fairly normally. She seems absolutely well enough to go home. Except she's asleep. And from our readings this time she's in so deep she's not about to wake up anytime soon."

Sondrine squeezed her daughter's hand.

"I was just looking back through her history. This is the third time she's been in?"

"Yes"

"Starting four years ago. When she was, what, three? Before that she was bright, alert, everything developing normally?"

"Hardly ever a sick day..."

"We always thought she was a star, way ahead of all her milestones. We talked about her being a genius. But then everybody does."

"Or an actress."

"Mer..." She pronounced it *mare*

"We did! You often said that."

"Ah well, she's certainly pretty enough. And she has no lack of confidence."

The doctor caught the faintest curl of accent in Sondrine's voice.

He looked at her face but couldn't quite see the daughter there. Remarkably beautiful in a golden skinned, dark-eyed European way. He thought of Juliette Binoche and Audrey Tatou.

In repose Sondrine's eyes carried centuries of sadness which she overcame when she talked to her husband, producing a reassuring glitter, although still with some edginess. They would be excitingly lustrous when she was truly happy.

"This started when you'd been up in the tropics?"

"Yeah, I'd been on a study tour for the Museum. Some smaller islands in Indonesia and the Philippines. When I was almost finished I asked Sondrine to bring Pixie up for a week to see some of the amazing stuff I'd come across. Insects, birds, flowers. I wanted her to see the colours and shapes and sounds she'd never experienced. Not a bad beach resort either..."

"She spent most of her time in the water. Like a bath, she said."

"She's a great swimmer. Can snorkel too."

"One day she brought me a lovely purple starfish. She put it back."

"It may or may not be related but we've spoken to our tropical medicine specialists. They've not seen anything quite like it. We thought initially along the lines of selective mutism, perhaps an extreme form of that. There are of course some 'sleeping" type sicknesses in Africa but all those tests are negative. In fact every test is negative. Nothing they know of that has this recurrence. Nothing that lingers in this way..."

"We were back almost a year and then one morning we couldn't wake her. No distress. No marks ... just asleep. Smiling even. We took here to emergency. Then we ended up here."

"That was the first time?"

"Yes."

"Then she recovered fully."

"Yes just before the next Christmas. The nurse came in one morning. It was a very warm morning ... she was looking out the window. Just like that, watching the birds in that tree."

"And six months later?"

"Yes, we had taken her home. 'What problem!', we all said. She went to kindy. She was back with her friends. Life of the party, as usual. Everything sweet as a nut. Then one morning in the middle of winter, there was no wake-up. Can't say I blame her. I don't want to get out of bed those mornings ..."

"Mer."

"So we were back in here again. And again this week."

"Well, we've done the same tests, and some new ones. All negative." The doctor turned the charts as though he was seeing them for the first time. Looking for the clue everyone had missed. That would be satisfaction. "The brain scan then was normal. Normal for someone enjoying a good sleep. Activity seemed to indicate a dreaming state. All I can say is she appears to be perfectly healthy. And as I said, growing as well as can be expected. Looking through again, I can't see anything here about family history. I'm surprised someone hasn't asked you that before. There's nothing on your side, Merac, or yours, Mrs Matrices, anything like this? Are you aware of anything at all out of the ordinary in your parents or grandparents?"

"We *have* been asked that before, and it turned out not to be important."

"We adopted her," said Sondrine.

"Oh. Adopted. OK."

The doctor looked at the forms again as though they should have told him that.

"And you don't know her family history?"

"We haven't pursued it."

The doctor looked up, preparing to be mildly quizzical. He caught Merac's eyes and looked back at the charts again.

"That's fine. That's fine," he said.

"What now?" asked Merac.

"We will have to move her from this bed. We'll have to discuss the options for a bed somewhere else. Judging from the last couple of ... events, she may be OK at home for some periods. But there's the feeding and the bathing..."

"I can do that. I've been doing that."

Her beauty was fierce-eyed but her lips and smile were as soft as her hand resting on her daughter's shoulder.

The doctor, who had this morning closed the eyes of one small boy, and told some other parents to steel themselves, had a moment of envy for the small gesture of love. He was separated from his wife, after she had admitted last year she could no longer stand by him. Although he was already starting paediatrics when they met and he had fully explained his life to come, she was more than unhappy, she was desolate. He could see it, and understand it.

On days off he told her the good stories, the team's successes, even the partly successful, the uplift of temporary triumphs, and the prolonging of happy family outcomes. All the weeks and months he gave people were precious to him ... but she could only weep at the deaths.

This case was neither one nor the other. Concerning, challenging but somehow not stressful. It felt like it should have a happy ending.

"I was wanting to talk to you about that. We want to take her home next weekend. Apart from everything else, there is this concert. She knows the music. Sondrine likes opera and she's taken Pix through the story of this one. It's a new production. Maybe something will get through..."

The doctor looked at Sondrine who raised one eyebrow.

"I... I don't see why not." he said. "I have to leave you now, but I'll report to the desk and you can take it from there."

The nurse smiled and left with him.

Merac dropped beside the head of the bed and kissed his daughter's forehead.

"No need to wake up just yet, darling. We'll get you home. Back in your room. And we'll show you a little surprise at the Opera House. Won't we, maman? A nice day out on Daddy's shoulders."

Sondrine crouched and looked at him across the sleeping face.

"She'll like that."

As his wife stepped away towards the door, the professor leaned down to his daughter once again.

"Not long now, darling. Just a couple of days."

In the quiet of the room the hesitant sound of a cicada starting up in the tree outside made Sondrine smile and she turned.

"Can you hear that?" Merac said, standing up. "You go. I'll sit with her till you're back."

Along the corridor heading for the garden, Merac passed a playroom. Looking in, he recognised a woman and her young son on a bright beanbag against the colourful wall. She was taking him through a picture book. There were so many meetings in a place like this. Everyone was always polite, maintaining their cheerfulness. He had seen tears, and heard choking voices. But never anger or intolerance. Quiet acceptance was the code for many visitors, but never for the staff. They were amazing. What did they say to themselves before every shift? How could they keep it up?

Over the years he had tried to play his part with those he passed. He remembered an undulating line of little children, a parade of hot-eyed parents against a dependable wall of white and blue coats. Few stayed clearly in his mind but he thought he had shared a laugh or two with this woman.

Her boy had no hair and a canula taped to the back of his left hand. He looked up and cracked a chuckle and pointed at Merac.

"Mandrake!" he squealed.

Merac remembered the meeting. Several meetings, a year or so ago. Shared in rooms and corridors, and in the garden one chilly day.

"Mandrake the Magician," Merac bowed. "Hullo, how's it going?"

"He's... he's good. It's looking OK." the mother answered.

"Show me a trick."

"No tricks" said Merac deeply "Only real magic here."

He crouched and tapped the boy's nose. He turned to the mother. "How on earth did he get 'Mandrake'? That's centuries old."

"Billy's grandpa used to talk about him. Dad did some tricks himself ... I think that's where it started."

"Where's the magic? I want to see it!"

The boy squirmed, grinning madly.

Merac only had some coins. And a pen. And a banknote.

But hey, the show must go on. He was very good at it.

The pen went up his nose and came out his ear. It came out mum's ear as well. Billy's nose had a tube in it. No room for a pen. So Merac bent the pen in half, soft as a piece of tinned spaghetti, then straightened it out for Billy to write his name on his wrist.

The banknote was folded and folded, rolled and rolled until it disappeared. Of course it came back. It was torn in half but somehow healed itself. The coins. Well, they were unstoppable. Coming and going like kids in a swimming pool on a hot summers' day. Where would they pop up next? In that ear? In that one? Noooo, it was under the bean bag all the time! Or was that the one in Billy's pocket.

"More, more!"

"Mandrake has to go and see some more kids. But this shiny dollar is going to disappear one more time and when it comes back, guess who owns it?"

"Billy!"

I hope that helped thought Merac as he made his way towards the sunlight.

The courtyard seemed different to him. Still had the big tree on one side, but new garden beds, paving and furniture. There were eight or nine children there. Some sitting silently with their parents, in chairs or wheelchairs. Some walking slowly. Very little evidence of bandages, plaster or splints. These were not injured children. They were sick. However three of them were quite chirpy looking up at the tree. Were they recovering? Recovered? Were they the siblings who did not yet feel the pain of finding out how lucky there were?

The cicada was strumming up again a half-hearted, scratchy gurgle.

Merac could hear he wasn't very high up and soon spotted him, just testing the equipment before he settled into a full song, reversing slowly down a thin branch towards the main trunk. The smooth cream and grey bark was marked with thin brown lines, as though someone had covered the tree with careless graffiti by taking to it with a sharp stylus, for multiple patches of undecipherable childish writing. The tree was a scribbly bark gum. *Eucalyptus haemstoma.* The lines are produced by an insect which lays its eggs under the top layer of bark. The larvae move upwards in a zig zag pattern which is revealed when the moth has left and the tree sheds its old bark.

Cicadas love the scribbly gum because they read and sing the lines.

A full chorus of cicadas is pretty much a one-note shriek. To most of them it's like an orchestra approaching the climax of a great symphony. Everyone is going full tilt. The conductor's upraised arms are encouraging them in their gallop to the finish. The heat of the day is heady encouragement. A full chorus can scare a flock of glittery-eyed birds and send them wheeling and deafened into the next park or paddock. In the midst of all this din, male cicadas save themselves from a serious deafening by relaxing the tension in their tympana. These sound receivers are also located under their abdomen quite close to the noise producing tymbals. Relaxing the tympana is the cicadas' equivalent of humans using earplugs.

But the tymbals are capable of tender and thoughtful passages too. Changes of key and volume don't come easily to of cicadas, but the more thoughtful ones like Gerry like to experiment.

Gerry can read scribbles and adjust his tone and phrasing to follow a whole trunkful of song.

Merac knew this because Gerry and others had told him.

It was first brought to his attention when he provided some small scribbly bark branches for the communal dinner in the boardroom. Obviously there were no scribbles on these thin shoots but some of the diners recognised them from their sap and started chatting about good times they'd had.

Back then he was fascinated as a sturdy Chocolate Soldier, Charles, took him through the process.

"Most of us have a limited pitch. We can move a note up and down a little but our sound is largely a function of the size we are born. Those little Tom Thumbs ... Tony looked up from his sapsuck when he heard his species mentioned ... have a much higher pitch, while big blokes like Frank and Ferdie those Floury Bakers have a much lower register. Reading the bark is mostly a timing thing. We follow the scribbles, swelling with the zigs, easing off on the zags, then a quick breath before we jump to the next scribble. It's great fun for us and quite demanding too. Most human ears would not pick it up. It would all sound the same. But we like to do it whenever a bunch of us find ourselves on a Scribbly Bark."

"Could you play a piece of music?"

"Like you do on the piano over there? No we can't just drop onto a note. We can slide up and down a little. I've heard that with practice some of the blokes can train themselves to hit a particular note, if it's not too far out of their register. It's all to do with the tension in our drums."

"Show me on this music over here." Merac extended his finger to carry Charles over to the piano.

He set him down on top where some sheets of music were lying and then played a note.

"OK, that's middle C."

Merac pointed to the music notation as he pushed the white key again. All round the room the cicadas looked up from their dinner. They love music of all kinds, especially the wind instruments, the swaggering blast from trumpets and cornets are right up their alley, but stringed instruments like the piano fascinate them.

"Can you play, I mean, sing that?"

"Whoa, way too low for me! I'm up here somewhere" said Charles raising a leg.

Charles scratched his way up to the head of the page, indicating several spaces above the top set of lines.

"How about High F. Right here." Merac indicated.

"Maybe on a low day. If I had a sore tymbal." Charles laughed. "Why High F?"

"Oh it's a special feature of a piece of music my wife and daughter really love."

Merac remembered all this clearly as he walked around the hospital tree and spoke up as the cicada above him came within seeing distance.

"Are you going to sing the scribbles for us?"

"I might." said the cicada guardedly. "Who's asking?

"My name's Merac. What's your name?"

"Giles"

"Have you been here long?"

"All my life. This is my tree. Lovely isn't it."

"Nice sap?"

"The best I've ever tasted. Actually, it's the only sap I've ever tasted."

"So life's OK?"

"Are you kidding? They've paved this over, look at that. From one side to the other. I was lucky to get out alive. I was right near the main trunk when my time came to emerge so I was able to crawl up in that small garden bed round the base. All my brothers and sisters who were living on the roots further out are still stuck down there. They've felt the stirring, woken up and headed for the surface. Then they've come bang up against the sandstone and that's it. All over. Good night, nurse. I don't think any of our kids will ever be able to go back down again. Another tree gone for good. Not a very nice thing for a place like this to do. These sick kids would be horrified if they knew."

"I'm sure they had their reasons. Boards of directors don't always think what happened seven years back. They weren't to know to expect you this year."

"Well they've ruined our life. It wouldn't be wise for us to stay here. From up the top I think I can spot a couple of gum trees in the distance, but it seems pretty built up as far as I can see. I'd really like our kids to grow up here but we can forget that."

"So you'll move on?"

"We'll have a go. This area, even though it's covered with buildings is not short of bird life. We might try a quick flight tonight when the birds are full of food and settling into their singing."

"You're a smart chap aren't you? I'd like you to meet a friend of mine. I could smuggle you out to somewhere you could start again. A big park in the city that will never be built over. How about that?"

"Could we bring my sister?"

"Of course, where is she?"

"Over there."

Holding onto the underside of a leaf that you would normally have called 'green' was the lovely face of another cicada. Now, *that's* green. Her glowing emerald made the scribbly bark's leaves look a plodding greenish grey.

Her huge compound eyes, not very old, met Merac's.

"What's your name?"

"Gwendolene."

Her jewels sparkled.

"Hullo, I've been talking to Giles and I'm thinking of taking you to a nice new home, where you can meet some new friends. There will be lots of fresh gum leaves too. Is that OK?"

"Thank you. I'd like that."

Merac extended his index finger for her to climb on, once again pleased at the politeness of his favourite creatures. How could you not love them?

Chapter Seventeen

"We'll keep this brief."

By that, Harold probably meant only one bottle of wine.

He had invited Robertson for a quick lunch. Very quick. Their mutual distaste would put anyone off their food, but they both had a reason to stomach each other for a meeting.

"Fine by me. I do have other things to do today. But Meg insisted."

"We're never going to be great mates, Roger, but we may be able to scratch each other's backs."

"Not too often, I hope," suppressing a shudder.

"Once will be enough."

Paul brought a bottle of red, overplaying the butler perhaps with his white gloves. He filled the huge Riedels halfway and left them. Robertson kept his eyes on Harold's. He ignored the view behind those hunched shoulders and watched carefully as his host took a generous slurp before wiping his mouth with the back of his hand. This set up was Harold's usual bargaining position. In his boardroom he had the head of the table placed closer than necessary to the window knowing the light from behind him would help conceal any giveaways in his eyes or lips. He knew he was a world-class liar but the mark of a champion is to keep giving yourself all the advantages and never giving the slightest break to your opponent.

"You had quite a career in the army. Then with our intelligence mob. Am I right?"

"You know you are."

"So you'd still know a few people in Canberra?"

"I keep in touch with some of them."

"One of them has been in touch with me."

"Really."

"Yes, it seems they want to see the old warhorse saddled up again."

"Me?"

Harold nodded.

"I think they would have been in touch with me first."

"Special set of circumstances, over which I have some control. Just came up in a meeting I had in Canberra last week. They knew I had been talking to you on another matter. This one, I gotta tell ya, has nothing to do with trees. Or Meg. That clear?"

Robertson tried a small sip of the red.

"The spooks agreed to let me take it from here. You're welcome to check it out. As I know you will."

"I will. Does that mean we have to take some time out now and regroup later? Another lunch to plan and fit in? Your butler and cook will be run off their feet." "If you insist on not trusting me we can do it right now. Paul will bring you a secure phone."

Paul slipped in and from the side table brought a red phone trailing a length of red cord.

A touch theatrical thought Robertson. I last saw that in a James Bond movie. The phone did however have a small code, a series of letters and numbers on a small plaque that he recognised. "Call your man."

No harm in playing along. Robertson tapped in a number.

"George. Rob. Yes a long time. Still it's a fine day anyway ... I would have to agree to that .... and again I would have to agree. Listen, I'm with Harold ... yes, that Harold. He tells me you might need me. He's told me nothing yet .... I will. I'll keep in touch."

"Everything OK?"

"Appears to be. He asked me to hear you out."

"OK. Here we go. As you know I spend a lot of time around the big end of this town. I can pick up the phone to anyone and they'll take my call. I also have necessary contact with the vermin that run around the bottom. My spies tell me that someone, some people, want to do something very naughty in this town. Involving destruction. Probably loss of life. It'll bring a big part of the joint to a halt.

Now, much as I love this fair city, I could just stay out of the way, ride this one out and let others deal with it, but if this .... this thing ....happens it will stuff up one of my pet projects. Big time. Something I have been working on for decades. Worth a lot, a lot, of money to me. I would hate that to happen."

"Are you asking me to run around with your vermin. I could suggest a few others more suited."

"No, the vermin this time are not your usual gutter dwellers. They are suit and tie blokes. Just like you and me. You probably sat next to one of the bastards at your club in the last couple of weeks."

Robertson took another sip. It was an excellent red. I really must thank Meg for pushing me into this meeting today, he thought. It is actually quite amusing observing this creature conduct his affairs. Of course, I will do a lot more checking, but this could just be a bit of fun and I haven't seen any downsides. Yet. I'm sure they will come. I'll make up my mind then.

Harold knew he had his man.

"You may be able to help stop this."

"How's that? Why not just call the police?"

"You've been watching too many of those Yank cop shows, Ralston. You should read more spy novels, or watch some of those terrific BBC series. You know it's never that simple. We don't talk to the cops. If we play our cards right we not only prevent the explosions, we get ourselves in with the people who matter and we advance our own position."

"Explosions?"

Harold looked hurt.

"Did I say that? No, we don't know that. Explosions. Dunno where that came from. Ah, Paul, nice tucker. Beautifully thawed. Our compliments to the freezer will you? Just kidding, Robbo. Paul is Cordon Blue. Before the next course, old chap, have you got that file we were looking at earlier?"

Paul went out and reappeared seconds later with a folder covered with a glossy clear plastic. He took

Robertson's plate and placed the folder right in front of him.

Harold continued:

"It's early days and we don't have everything. In fact I don't want to show you everything just yet, but have a squizz at what's there and see if I am not right to be alarmed and let me know if you reckon a man of your background couldn't help."

Robertson opened the folder. There were just a few memos, emails and letters some of them original, some copies. There were sections of plans of the city and some drawings and diagrams.

"The Opera House?" said Robertson holding up one page.

"Looks like it could be."

Robertson read a few of the notes in more detail and finally looked up."It all seems rather vague only peripheral stuff. Nothing positive, and I don't see any timing on any of these."

"Of course, they're too smart to write any specifics down, but we have some verbal on that. A few words on the street."

"How much do you know you are not telling me?"

"Not much more than that. But what we have heard could be corroborated by some of the answers you might get if you talk to some of the names on those pages."

"I've heard of a few of them. Met one or two... what do you want me to do."

"There's a long way to go. A lot more for you to do. But you could start with just catching up with these characters. See what they're up to. See if they have any intentions involving planning and construction around the CBD. They'll open up to you."

Paul took the folder back and left the room. Harold was ready to sum up.

"I reckon you just keep your eyes and ears open for a while. We'll talk soon when we can go deeper and use your skills more specifically. OK"

"Is that it?"

"Can you think of anything else we can do today."

"I suppose not."

"I want to show you something on your way out. I'll come down with you."

Harold used a security pass allowing them to take the lift right down to the first carpark level. He led the way to a bay near the steel-grilled main gate. He opened the door of the silver Mercedes.

"Have a sit."

Harold knew Roberston had been quite a successful car racer and rally driver, it had been part of his cover in his overseas postings after his army service. He also knew he had been a member of various Mercedes enthusiast clubs and was now a committee member of the club in Sydney.

He knew a soft spot when he read about one and now he pushed right into it.

"Been in one of these?"

"No...actually. It's the S65?"

"Right, the AMG. If you haven't been in one then you haven't driven one. Until now that is. Here you go. I just thought a man like you might appreciate a quick trip around the block."

"Er... thanks. I would."

Harold stepped back. He raised his hand and the steel door began to rise. He stepped back holding up his mobile phone for Robertson to see.

"I just have to have a quick word with this bloke. Take it onto the driveway. I'll join you there."

The traffic wasn't too bad in the early afternoon, but they still couldn't raise much more than a purr for most of the ten minutes with the exception of a very brief blast up Macquarie Street from the roundabout down near the Opera House car park.

"Go you good thing, Robbo!" chortled Harold as he pretended to hide from the acceleration with his head under the dashboard.

Back at the garage Robertson guided the vehicle effortlessly into its spot.

Harold stuck out his chubby hand.

"Good, it's been a fine day. You'd have to agree with that."

Smiling broadly, Harold didn't mind giving away that he now knew some of Robertson's code words. He didn't mind what Robertson thought or did from now on. He had what he wanted.

"I have a meeting. Thanks for coming in. I'll be in touch."

Back upstairs Paul came in to clear after their visitor had left.

"How did we go, sir?"

"Nailed it."

"In what way, sir?"

"We've now got CC footage of him driving my car. Right out of my secure car park. I certainly didn't give him permission to take it. I'll swear that on a stack of bibles. Everyone knows only my driver touches that thing. How did he get hold of it? They'll find out he's a spy. They'll guess he worked his way into my organisation. Got hold of the keys or a copy of the keys whatever those spooks do. Not quite sure how we'll use it, I was planning to drive to the carpark myself. Might come in handy though. Maybe we can say he took the car earlier and put the bomb in there. Or dropped it off. Or did a practice run. We'll think of something. He should also be on the Opera House cameras. That will be incriminating in some way if I say I never knew he had my car."

"So when do we activate him?"

"We don't need him to do any more. We've already got all we need. We've now got his fingerprints all over those pages that the blokes behind the explosion were using in their planning. They'll turn up after the incident. Somehow they'll find their way into the right hands. We've got more prints on that red phone and you've got a bloke who can lift them and place them on any other device, haven't you? We've got few spares on the wine glass too."

"His work here is done?"

"Aww, we'll send him up a few alleys and dead ends. He'll be noted by the right people as being interested in this whole thing, maybe even a player. Any more wine?"

"I'd have to open another bottle."

"Have we run out of corkscrews?"

Chapter Eighteen

"There used to be a lot of boozers in Sydney like this. This is pretty well the last of them."

"It's nice," said Paul. "A bit like an English pub."

"Hear that sound?"

Paul could hear the hum and snort of cars outside, but in here were just some quiet voices and the clink of pub glasses. Some sounds from a kitchen somewhere round the corner. That was it.

"What am I listening for?"

"Pokies."

"I can't hear them."

"That's because there are none."

"No poker machines. In a Sydney hotel. Are you serious? Not out the back?"

"None at all. The bloke who has owned this pub for the last twenty years won't have a bar of them. He has said over and over again people come to my pub to drink, eat and talk. That's what a neighbourhood pub is for."

"He'd be going broke without them."

"No way. Lunch time's a bit quiet. But his kitchen does well. Nighttime the place is packed. Locals. Young people. Good music. Classical. Jazz. Blues. Old rock and roll ... always quiet in the background..."

"Sounds perfect."

"He has some interesting beers. He was one of the first to do decent wine by the glass. People round here love him."

"You'll have a drink yourself, Barry?"

"Does Dolly Parton sleep on her back?"

"I'd heard it as 'Does Dolly Parton get backache?'"

"Same diff. Poor kid, they pick on her don't they. She's a really nice lady they reckon."

"What'll it be?"

"Reschs. Schooner."

"Same as Guy."

"Where is the bastard? You did tell him the East Sydney. This is not his regular pub. He could be anywhere if you didn't make that clear. "

"I definitely said the East Sydney at three."

"Right. Not in a hurry are you? Getting yourself a drink?"

"Two schooners of Reschs" Paul said to the girl. They watched as she poured. A strong flow into the angled glass until three quarters full. Snap off the tap. Put that one down on the perforated drip try. Do the same with the second one. Put it down and take up the first one to top it up. Then the second. Each with a perfect half inch of smooth white froth on top. Place them on the bar towel as the dark gold liquid steadies itself around the delicately rising bubble chains.

"Poetry, isn't it."

"It looks nice."

"They always do a good one here."

They moved to a small table in the corner. Above them the dark green walls were almost covered floor to ceiling, end to end, with old beer and spirit posters, signs and mirrors. It is a nice pub thought Paul. His companion took an almighty gulp of his beer. About a quarter of it, Paul estimated as he took his modest sip.

"How do they do it for the price!" rasped Barry Boomgate with an exaggerated shudder, and not for the first time. In fact he said it every time he took his first sip. On a hot day like today, he really meant it. He often followed up with: 'If it was a tenner a glass you'd still drink it.' But not today. He was still not quite sure what was to be discussed, but when Paul had called him mentioned Guy's name and suggested they meet, Barry had chosen his own ground suspecting something of importance might be on the table, possibly even something illegal. He didn't want to choose a regular haunt, preferring somewhere quiet but not hidden, busy but not crowded, at a time there was little chance of seeing anyone he knew.

"Known Guy for long?" asked Barry.

"I've only me him once."

Another deep pull on the beer. Paul took two sips. Mustn't get too far behind.

"He's an interesting bloke, Guy. What's left of him."

Barry laughed croakily at his joke, checking to see how Paul took it.

"This'd be something to do with explosives I take it."

"Er, yes. Something."

"Cagey, aren't ya?"

"Well I thought we might wait till Guy gets here."

"It might also have something to do with where I work?"

"Something."

"Very cagey."

"I'd rather wait till Guy is here. When it is all explained I believe you will find it a very interesting and profitable proposition."

"Sounds great. Meanwhile I gotta grab a ciggy. Can't do it in here. Back in a sec."

Barry left his half full glass on the table, pulled a pack of Winfields from his pocket and slipped out the door onto the footpath under the awning and the sign that said *East Sydney Hotel originally known as The Shamrock Hotel 1856.* He walked a few steps away and lit up. Paul studied the walls as he tried manfully to sip his beer down to half way before Barry came back. He hoped Guy wouldn't be too long. On his own, he was not at ease with these 'real Aussies' these 'true blue battlers' these 'salt of the earth' as the politicians called them, although, God knows, he'd had plenty of experience with Harold's coarse manner. He would be much more comfortable when he had outlined the task, dangled the obscene amount of money, obtained the agreement and retired to his flat in Darling Point with some Chablis and Stravinsky.

Paul was very good at doing what he had to do, he really enjoyed it but he had to do it because of what Harold had on him.

Above a shelf lined with bottles of decent wine he focussed on a framed poster that didn't seem to be advertising any particular alcohol. The print itself seemed quite old and faded and Paul had some trouble making out just what he was seeing. It looked like a drawing of a group of mice around a mousetrap. Oh no. It was! The one in the foreground was trapped by the neck, not quite dead by the look of it and all the others were queuing up to ...oh that's awful!

"My favourite poster" said Guy, suddenly silently standing beside him.

How did a man who spent his life in such a roar of noise and smoke manage such stealth?

"Where's Barry?"

"Outside. Having a cigarette."

"Silly bugger should have given it up years ago. I did. Mind you I didn't have much left to hold a pack with. Let alone a lighter."

Guy sat down with some difficulty. Now he was so close Paul could hear the metallic scrapes and squeaks as he eased his restructured limbs onto the seat.

"Should I summon Barry?"

"Nah. He'll be in by the time you fetch me a beer."

Over the next few schooners Paul explained the proposal. Guy was already signed up to provide the 'decorations' for the 'party'. For the 'celebration' to go off perfectly it required a person to not notice, and indeed make sure no one else noticed, some 'presents' wired into very precise spots against columns and along the cliff near the entrance of the Opera House car park.

That person would be paid very well, provided with a very decent alibi to be away from his post for the appropriate period, and then go into retirement somewhere up the coast to fish himself silly and drink like a fish for the rest of his life.

Barry Boomgate was that person.

After another three schooners, Paul was outside in Cathedral Street, leaving his now co-conspirators to enjoy a quiet drink by themselves. He hoped they would behave themselves. He recalled one of his grandfather's wartime slogans: "Loose lips sink ships." We don't want any of that happening around here. Although what we are doing has nothing to do with ships so that's really silly. Paul tried to keep a grip on himself.

As he nearly stepped in front of a car which fortunately had slowed right down for the Stop sign he realised that he was, as he would put it, quite tipsy. Shickered would be Barry's word for it.

He could on occasions match Harold glass for glass with a good red over lunch or dinner, but half a dozen schooners of icy cold beer in a short space of time where now beginning to catch up with him. He started looking for a cab and noting nothing immediate he contemplated walking back to Macquarie Street. Might sober him up. If he found a cab maybe he should take it straight home. He knew Harold would be waiting for his report, but in his current condition perhaps he had better phone it in.

He adjusted his pocket handkerchief where he had concealed the recording mike. He was sure he had brokered a good deal. Barry and Guy, whose backgrounds Paul knew through his extensive checking indicated a history of dirty deeds, immorality and greed, had been quite blunt in their demands. When they learned the full extent of the project, they knew the law would do a lot of swarming, and although accepting Paul's assurances that Harold had the power to keep the coppers in their boxes, or at least divert them, they knew this had to be a huge payday. After Paul had made his first offer (high but with plenty of padding left) they considered the extent of their involvement. Emboldened by subsequent Reschs they asked for more money. Running through the logistics they could each see a way of getting away with it, and with the money now on offer, getting away rich.

Exactly how many millions Harold had riding on every deal, Paul never knew. Certainly it was his job to liaise with lawyers, accountants, councils and builders as they drew up essential paperwork, however there was always a substantial percentage of black money that he could only guess at.

But there was no doubt this was a big one and Harold had to have the job done and done well with loose ends tied. He was happy to part with serious cash, more than serious to the likes of Barry and Guy. The day had not cost a million dollars but you wouldn't buy too many of Harold's Mercedes with the change from that amount.

As a cab with its light on came towards him Paul waved it down. He would take it home. He poured himself a glass from one of the better bottles in his wine fridge and spun through the recording of the

163

conversation in the East Sydney, replaying some sections to make sure everything was clear and precise. He phoned Harold.

The 'decorations' would arrive on time. The 'presents' would be suitably wrapped and the 'party' would erupt on the evening of the following Saturday.

Chapter Nineteen

The City of Sydney is host to three notable winds.

Great friends or foes if you are a sailor on the Harbour's waters.

But a much more serious consideration if your craft weighs only a few grams and your sails are the size of cigarette papers.

Of course a wind can come from any point of the compass, but Sydney's Big Three have earned their names and each has its own personality with variables of strength, temperature and persistence.

The Nor'easter is a summer wind coming in off the Pacific Ocean. Usually starting softly in the morning it can whip itself up to a bluster, often sleeping again at night to wake the next day. Surfers on the ocean beaches can bless it for the swells it brings although it can also cause and upwelling of colder water which might even call for a wet suit in summer. It can of course also sweep moisture in off the sea and bring substantial rain. A Black Nor'easter is a storm squall that can form from nothing in less than an hour and swamp the city and its citizens.

The Southerly is nicknamed the Southerly Buster when it arrives in such a hurry it flattens unwary harbourcraft in minutes. Many a young dingy sailor has had if not his first but his most violent capsize and possible need for rescue when only a few hundred metres from his home shore. When you are working hard racing in a swarm of your peers it is not always possible to look up to the south for the leading edge, the roll cloud, of wind you really don't want.

With small variations east or west of true south, the Southerly can come from over water or land depending on the season and can bring violent whipping rain. Or in Winter it might blow for days bringing volumes of numbing cold air from the snow on the Alps.

The Westerly comes from the parched red country which stretches from a few hundred kilometres west of Sydney for another few thousand kilometres to the West Australian coast. A Westerly is a breath of hot air. It fans bushfires, or where there is no bush to burn, it kills gardens and old people, lifts carpets in hallways if you forget to shut the doors and frazzles parents trying to get small sweating children to sleep.

As Gerry cleared the edge of the cliff above the Opera House he wasn't aware of any wind.

His eyes were on the shining structure above him. He had poor long vision. The little eyes on the outside of his head saw only a sheet of white. His other central eyes, the ocelli, the three jewels, helped maintain equilibrium and control.

'It's huge,' thought Gerry as he worked hard with his beating wings for the height to take himself over the biggest sail of the Opera House.

He could have gone around it, but he wanted to keep his line of sight towards Admiralty House.

(Merac had cautiously suggested that if he ran out of puff, he could catch his breath on Kirribilli Point then cross to Kurraba Point then on to the Pool). Besides, he felt full of vigour. Maybe burning off a little excess fuel would not be a bad thing.

Perhaps his real reason was to inspect the main sail. He knew from conversations with other city cicadas, particularly those who lived in the Botanic Gardens that the Opera House was a place of pilgrimage for them. It dominated their skyline. The young males would dare each other to fly across and touch its swelling sides. Many had not returned, adding to the sense of awe it inspired. 'This is a Quest!' thought Gerry. 'I must learn and take in all that I can. For those who may come after.'

There was another possible reason a hero might not acknowledge. On the forecourt of the Opera House Gerry had noticed some large white birds. He had never seen them so close. They were seagulls, and he had never given them much thought before. When they were pointed out to him by friends at the water's edge of the Gardens he could see how cleanly and whitely they carried themselves. With disturbingly big red feet and beaks. Formidable. As he watched them effortlessly swoop and swerve he thought you could well design a fighter aircraft around their muscular curves. His assumption then and now had to be that they ate only seafood. But he wasn't sure.

'It has nothing to do with bravery,' thought Gerry. 'Just prudence. An eaten hero gets nothing done.'

As he climbed he was grateful to discover a gentle breeze up his backside, slightly warm. This was not one of Sydney's notable winds but a light sou'wester which sometimes blew benignly on summer mornings. Very pleasant for early risers around the Harbours many inlets. It would almost certainly be replaced by one of the Big Three as the day wore on.

He stayed on the sunnier side of the big sail. The slowly warming tiles on the mighty roof seemed to be giving him some uplifting air drafts. Much closer now, Gerry could focus on the outlines of their geometry. So that is man-made, eh? He couldn't think of a pattern in nature he had seen to match it. A cicada's natural world has very few straight lines so this feast of interlocking units straight-edged but conforming and contributing to a swelling curve were fascinating to him. Each tile was almost a square but wasn't. Each was almost flat but wasn't. Geometry was not Gerry's strong point so his little brain soon gave up. He would never have to design and build an opera house. He had much more important things to do.

But he would take up the dare of the Gardens' cicadas and touch the monster.

Lower, lower, lower. With his eyes full of whiteness he made contact. There was no way his tiny claws could get any purchase on the glossy ceramics. He slid quickly down the face. The joints offered some roughness with a chance of grip. By the fourth tile below the one he'd hit he managed to hang on. Not feeling sufficiently anchored to fold and settle, he let the breeze off the tiles give some reassuring lift to his partly closed wings. He looked around.

'Can't see what they see in this.' he thought. 'Not that mystical. Just uncomfortable. I *thought* there was something funny about those Gardens cicadas. They've been sucking on too many exotic plants'

He let go and took off again, this time heading more easterly that he realised. As he cleared the edge he became aware of the dark thrusting crescent of the Harbour Bridge to his left, twice as high as the sail he had just left. From this angle the arch displayed more delicacy in its steel outlines than he'd imagined ... more of man's ingenuity.

'That's another piece of geometry I don't want to tangle with.'

He looked down and realised he was over the water. Now this is serious.

His destination he knew should be straight ahead but he couldn't make it out. Not only was he in unfamiliar territory, his long vision was not that good.

"Head towards the rising sun and you can't miss it." Cir Franklin had grandly directed him the night before.

Gerry had no trouble seeing the sun. He headed for it, straight and level, with a modest tailwind some fifty metres above the lazy water. There was not nearly enough wind to cause any waves, scarcely any sparkle this time of day but there were patches of froth and churned white trails from the occasional ferry or pleasure boat, gradually settling through pale blue, mid blue and back to the deep blue/green of the undisturbed surface.

'Travelling well.' thought Gerry.

Just several minutes into his journey he noticed some kind of island coming up underneath. Not much bigger than the part of the Opera House he had flown over. Mostly rocky, but with a strip of green grass. A slight fringing of white water where small waves lapped at it. That's a big round tower at one end. And walls with battlements.

'Hmmm, that's not what I expected.' he thought. 'There we no islands on the course Merac plotted for me. Where am I?'

Even if he had a shoulder, he couldn't look over it while he kept flying, but he was sure the Opera House was still directly behind him. The sun was certainly still in front of him. He couldn't be that far out.

It was still early in the day. The plan drawn up the previous night allowed for an easy morning crossing. This to be followed by some exploration and investigation. The area to be covered was not huge. Gathering the necessary information should be easily accomplished. Then there should be plenty of time for a little sapsucking - there were several species of eucalypts on the far shore Merac knew from experience - to top up his strength. And then there should even be time for a little rest before setting off for a late afternoon return crossing. This because Gerry would now be able to aim for the setting sun. No problems at all in heading back to his point of origin.

For such an Important Quest Merac and Cir Franklin had made it sound surprisingly easy.

Then why am I suddenly finding myself pointing at an island I didn't know existed and I am only a short way into my journey? Am I lost already? Will I have to ask for directions?

Sure! No problem. Excuse me, is there anyone here on this little island speaks Cicada?"

Gerry aimed down towards the top of the flagpole.

"I should be safe there for a minute."

But he missed it. Cicadas weigh so little that a sudden slight breeze out in the open like this can throw them off. He continued down to a carved grey stone wall, then jumped quickly on to a patch of grass. "My favourite colour" he thought, "Should provide some camouflage while I work out where I am. "

Gerry tried walking through the grass. It was hopelessly slow and uncomfortable. He hadn't seen any seagulls on his way down, so he decided to take to the air. In a series of fluttering hops he approached the big round tower at the far end of the island. The secrets of this island had to be in there. Perhaps even a map to guide him on his way.

There were a few small square openings in the roughhewn sandstone walls. Gerry tried to see what was inside but his view was restricted and unhelpful.

He flew around and saw there was a large door at the base of the tower where a paved area led away to a clear plastic marquee set up on the side of the island facing back to the city. Inside there appeared to be a restaurant with tables and chairs set up for lunch. They're unlikely to have any decent saplings on the menu.

This early in the morning there was not much activity. It would be a couple of hours before the first of the ferries arrived bringing tourists for morning tea.

Gerry crouched on a warming stone wall.

This was truly depressing after such a felicitous start. I can't really go on, even if I head straight for the sun. I know I have to go in that direction, but I also know from Merac's map it's a big harbour and I could end up anywhere. On the other hand I can't just sit here. No one to ask. No one to talk to. So this is what being on a Quest is all about. I don't want to let people down but it seems I'm not very good at it.

Gerry scrabbled sideways as he heard a louder engine noise above the steady thrum of maritime sound carrying from all directions across the water.

From his clawhold on the tower he could see a bright yellow water taxi tracing a tight arc to bring itself into the steps of the white painted wharf. Apart from the driver, a jolly giant of a man with a shaved head there were four other people on board. The driver jumped off and tied up. He held out his huge palm to help one of the ladies onto the first step just above water level. They only had a couple of steps to reach the ramp which led up to the paved surface.

"There you go" said the driver. "Mind the step. She's pretty calm at the moment, so you'll be right. Hey Meg, do you want me to wait or come back?"

"We should be around an hour. Can I call when we've nearly finished. Is there another job you can do, Andy?"

"Might squeeze in a quickie. You've got my mobile haven't you?"

"Indeed I do."

"Sweet. Catch ya."

The taxi chugged away from the wharf, with a belch or two of black smoke bubbling in the water, then roared up to speed and scooted back towards the Quay.

Meg had been delegated to look after the Visiting Conductor and his Wife for a quick visit to the island which they had noted with interest when taken on a harbour cruise their first day in Sydney. He was a native of Dublin and the Martello tower reminded him of the one in Sandygate made famous in the greatest of all novels.

"This way" said Meg almost skipping up the ramp on her well toned legs. She was not at all unhappy to be given this task. An early start on the Harbour was a luxury of time she could not always afford. On a beautiful day like this she had allowed all morning, with lunch, if that is what the maestro and his wife wanted. She had heard that the Conductor had had some kind of military upbringing or career so she had invited Robertson along as well, thinking his impeccably soldierly background would make a perfect fit. She had quite liked the Wife at their first meeting earlier in the week and was looking forward to showing off her knowledge of Fort Denison. This was the island that they, and Gerry, were now on.

They were met by the resident caretaker wearing a white shirt with the badge of a National Parks and Wildlife Service. He knew more about the history of the island and its tower than anyone, but on this occasion he was happy to defer to the determined handsome woman he had welcomed on these kinds of private tours before.

As they walked past the marquee up towards the lawn she began brightly.

"This is the cafe where we could have had lunch if we were here a little later, but we have more things to do in the city so I thought we'd find somewhere more salubrious in there if that's OK with you? Yes?"

Gerry watched and listened. The lady he now knew as Meg was wearing a bright green blouse with a ruffling kind of collar tied in a bow which draped a little way across her back and down over her bosom. She had chosen it in deference to her guests' nationality.

If you were looking to match the green of a Greengrocer you could not do better than that.

The small group was about to pass right beside Gerry's position on the stone wall. Robertson, who had been alerted to fill conversational gaps with military chat deemed to be of interest to the Conductor when not talking music, had stopped to point out across the water the boats tied up at the Garden Island naval base The grey hulls and superstructure were dominated by the huge T shape of the 250ton Hammerhead Crane crane that was "the largest in the Southern Hemisphere" built to service World War II warships.

The ladies stopped too, looking slightly more to the right as Meg pointed out the promontory known as Mrs Macquarie's Chair.

Gerry seized his chance hoping Robertson's booming voice would cover the flutter of tiny wings.

Success.

For the next half hour neither Meg nor the rest of her party noticed the tan coloured eyes with tiny black specks peering out from the folds of loose green silk around her neck.

"This is the Martello tower." said Meg as they passed through the heavy wooden door "One of the last ever built in the British Empire, and the only one in Australia. Sean, you mentioned the ones near Dublin so you would be aware they were built all around the British Isles as a defence against the French in the early nineteenth century."

Robertson intervened. "The design is based on a tower finally captured by the British after it resisted days of shelling at Mortella Point during the Corsican campaign. They were so impressed by its strength they took the design back to England. The name was subsequently misspelled ..."

Meg leaped in. "The walls are six metres thick at the water line and three metres thick at the top.

'Not quite' thought the caretaker. 'But close enough.'

"This one was built in the 1850s when they feared a Russian invasion, but by the time it was completed the hostilities and the threat were over. I'm told the big guns have never been fired in anger. Although the small gun is fired every day at one o'clock."

"So you can set your mobile phone by it" said the Conductor cheekily.

The tour went on.

"Did I hear someone referring to this charming place as Pinchgut? That's not very charming." the Conductor's Wife asked in her mild Irish lilt.

"Ah. Glad you mentioned that. The original island was actually quite steep and rocky and in the early days of the colony it was used as solitary confinement to discipline convicts. As none of them could swim they were marooned here for days with only bread and water. So they came to call it 'pinchgut'. They had a gibbet erected here for hangings too. So the men were none too fond of it.

Gerry clung to his silken ride as Meg pirouetted. Her turnings and her focus were now his too. He was locked in. His mind was alert for anything that could tell him where they were and in which direction his Quest lay.

'There' thought Gerry. 'A map of the Harbour. On that wall. Please! Please!'

"Where did we go on that fine boat the other day? I have not much of a head for geography. Is this the Harbour here?" The Conductor was walking towards the map.

'Yes! Yes!' thought Gerry.

It was as easy as that. It could not have been spelled out more clearly than Meg did, her jewelled fingers tracing the precise information Gerry needed.

"We started at Circular Quay. Out past the Opera House, across to Admiralty House and Kirribilli House across Neutral Bay, past Cremorne Point and on to the Zoo. Fort Denison is here. We passed it on the way out and on the way back ..."

'Gotcha!' Gerry shouted in his thoughts. 'There's my Pool right over there. I was aiming too far to the right when I left the white sails. If I take it a bit more to the left, I'm there. You beauty! Thanks Meg! Thanks Sean!'

He almost wiggled with joy but froze when a scarlet fingertips came right up in his face and adjusted the folds of the silk. Could she feel him there? He couldn't make himself any smaller.

"Could we have some coffee? Is your cafe open yet?"

"I'm sure we can rustle something up."

They walked out of the tower and strolled to the marquee, where the caretaker led them in.

"We'll be rolling up the sides before the first guests arrive, it's such a lovely day. Not a breath of wind."

"There may be some weather coming in this afternoon." said Robertson, donning his sailor's hat.

Gerry was anxious to be on his way. He had been taking his sightings as soon as they stepped into the sunlight. He knew exactly which parapet he would launch himself over. But he was not in a position to take off before they moved inside the marquee, the folds of silk that Meg had rearranged were now covering his wings. What're a few more minutes, anyway? She would have to phone for the water taxi and as soon as she steps outside it will just take a quick crawl and away I go. It wouldn't matter if she felt him then. He'd be on the wing and gone. Maybe this big chap is going to come up with some more information about the weather which may be helpful for the return journey. I'd love a quick slurp of sap but there doesn't seem to be a single tree on the island.

I'll have to settle for watching them take a tea break.

They sat round a table and a smart young girl came out to take their orders.

Robertson leant back in his chair and turned to the Conductor. One military man to another.

"So tell me, Sean, you spent some time in the Army, I 'm told. Unusual transition for a military man to move so successfully into music, eh? I did some years in England, taught at Sandhurst for a spell, but I never came across any officers who left to take up conducting an orchestra. Must say I couldn't play a note myself."

"I was a captain in the IRA." Sean said with a smile. "I believe I was your enemy. As a matter of fact, I believe I still have that rank. Am I still your enemy?"

Robertson was speechless. Meg had never seen him like this before. He was flushed in the face, breathing quite hard. He had once told her he he'd lost comrades all over the world, but she knew he had lost a particular friend in Northern Ireland.

"Jaisus, Sean" said the Conductor's wife quietly. Her eyes were wide.

"It's OK, Mary." He rested a hand on her arm. "This is between gentlemen."

Even Gerry caught the whiff of gunpowder in the air and had to hold himself still. If he had been outside the marquee this would seem a perfect time to hop it. But now he had a front row seat.

"I lost a good friend in Belfast."

"I lost many."

They stared at each other. The women held their breath. Robertson leaned forward, not threatening but controlled. He said quietly.

"I despised your methods, sir, and always will, but as I am myself of Irish descent, I had some,

I wouldn't quite say sympathy, but some understanding of your cause."

"You don't look like the wild colonial boy."

"My family has been here five generations."

The conductor sat back in his chair.

"May we agree it was a long time ago?"

"Are you sure you are not finished yet?"

"I am. I am very sure. I know there are others still plotting and probing, but I think I'll let my offspring watch it unfold. It will be up to them."

Robertson leaned back.

"I would agree with you on that. Old men should not plan their children's fights."

"Would you like to have a talk some time?"

"About music, about Sydney, about wine and food ... but not about war."

"As you will. I am here for another seven weeks."

"You could take him to the Mercantile." Meg offered. This pub in the Rocks was rumoured to have harboured IRA fugitives during the height of the Troubles.

Before Robertson could chide her for her mischief, Sean cut in, ramping up his brogue for a more sinister effect: "I've already been there briefing the lads over a pint or two. The Guinness is more than acceptable."

"A pint of plain is your only man." quoted Robertson

"You like it?" Sean was smiling.

"Indeed, especially with Sydney rock oysters."

"I will have to try that."

"You're on."

The coffee and pastries arrived and they talked about the music Sean would be conducting. Nothing Irish. Nothing British. All safely Continental: Italian, French and German.

"How *did* you become a conductor, Sean?" Asked Meg hoping the air was now well and truly clear of rancour.

"Well then. That's a story in itself. I had cause to apply to attend the Dublin College of Music. It was necessary to sit a rigorous examination."

"Of course."

"I was quite dismayed by the first question on the paper. It was in two parts. It was something along these lines: ' *A) Of Mozart's 41 symphonies only two are in a minor key. What are the numbers of these symphonies, what is the key, and in the later work what is the submediant major employed in the second movement. In respect of Mozart's early symphonies, discuss...'*

Meg hung on every word. Her lips were actually moving as her mind spun deliciously racing to fill in some of the answer herself. She knew she could do it.

The conductor's wife sat back expressionless. Robertson hovered somewhere in between.

The conductor finished his story.

'*... or, B) draw a potato.'*

Meg was aghast. Robertson got it first, catching the wife's eye who gave him a twinkle.

Robertson turned to his companion kindly.

"Meg."

She saw the smiles and the penny dropped. She hooted and didn't stop for 20 seconds. The others sat back enjoying her.

Tissuing her eyes back to dry, she touched the conductor on the knee. 'May I tell that?"

"Any time you like, my dear lady."

When they stepped outside Robertson looked at the sky.

"What say you, Skipper?" asked the Conductor.

"Quite warm and muggy already. Could be a storm in it this afternoon. Possibly a southerly ..."

'Uh oh' thought Gerry still hanging in there. 'I'd better get a wriggle on. A quick Quest is a good Quest. Over and back before nightfall seems like the best idea.'

He crawled quickly from the last of the green folds that held him and with one bound he was free, whirring past Meg's ear.

"What was that!"

"Do you have leprechauns here? It looked like a little puff of green magic."

Chapter Twenty

Gerry whirred his way up to cruising height. The slight sou'westerly was still pushing him along. He looked down at the water as a sailing boat crossed underneath him, an older sloop with stained sails set tight, a gentle hiss from the water stroking the length of its golden varnished sides. In the cockpit was a couple with their children, the kids in red lifejackets, the mother handing out some kind of snack, the father with his eyes on the mainsail. It was a gentle morning. No need to tack for a while.

A mumble of conversation and they were gone. Gerry was on his own again with the green water below.

'I've never been in water' thought Gerry 'Maybe a shallow puddle in the rain. I wonder what it feels like.' He kept his eyes straight ahead, this time confident in his direction. 'I'll try not to find out today.'

In the distance, in reality less than a kilometre, he could make out a low strip of land smudged with green tapering to a ferry wharf at its harbour end. All along its length were blocks of apartments, none as tall as some he could see across the Harbour on the southern shore. Fortunately nearer the water there was a decent strip of grass and a variety of trees in front of the buildings. He was on course. He knew that halfway along the Point was his goal. The McCallum Pool.

'Easy peasy' he thought, using a phrase Merac was fond of. A fluff of wind lifted him higher and there it was. A rectangle of light blue, as though someone had cut a mat of sky and set it at the edge of the green harbour waters. As he homed in he saw the picket fence, the narrow boardwalk, and the quaint little building on the end that housed the pump. There was a variety of large trees thrusting each in their distinctive shape from the sloping grass on the landward side. Some of them overhung the Pool, shadowing it this time of day. The evening would make those lawns a lovely warm place to watch a sunset. Hardly a ripple washed up against the concrete walls and the oyster-covered rocks either side. The tide was quite high. There was one woman in the pool breaststroking gracefully, two others standing waist deep and chatting, and one man with a smile as broad as his body as he rinsed himself under the freshwater shower. His tanned chest swelled as he took deep breaths after completing his laps of the pool. He had done the same number as usual but he felt really good on the last two.

Running his fingers through his streaming hair, snorting the last of the salt water out of his nose and rubbing his eyes, he looked out at the sight that for thirty years had made these early starts, if not always the high point, at least the springboard that launched him energised into his day.

Before him, across the shining levels of water, was the vista of Sydney Harbour. Not at all as Arthur Phillip would have seen it in 1788 when he described it as 'one of the finest harbours in the world – in which a thousand sail of the line may ride in the most perfect security.'

And not much like the view that prompted Joseph Conrad over a century later to describe it as 'one of the finest, most beautiful, vast and safe bays the sun had ever shone upon'

Although, if you wished, a couple of kilometres behind the man in the shower, on some of the Harbour's preserved headlands you could see the same massed green/grey eucalypts and low scrub clinging to tumbled and weathered sandstone that would have bemused northern eyes centuries ago.

As he sluiced the fresh water through his Speedos, he looked at modern Sydney.

It was all built up as far as his eyes could see. To his left across a kilometre of water, the cute outline of the toy castle of Fort Denison; behind which he picked up the band of green from Mrs Macquarie's Chair all the way right across the water's edge of the Gardens. Behind was the backdrop of the central business district. Tall structures bunched together, but it was not quite Manhattan. If you focussed you could make out a jagged mismatch of heights widths and architectural styles: squared off, round topped and pyramided with extended masts, tubes and poles.

Ironically if you softened your gaze this proud upthrust of modernity so carefully calculated and constructed by man began to look like a random ridge of a mountain thrown up by a restless earth and weathered over the millennia.

The right hand end of the green strip was chopped suddenly short by the dramatic leap of the Opera House. From this angle he saw a starker view than most visitors see - two sets of triple tiered teeth, sharp peaked with white but presenting the darkness of their glassed undersides. It reminded him less of the white sails of the boats on the surface of these waters, but more the jaws of the sharks that cruised constantly under it.

To his immediate right the boats anchored in the tapering Shell Cove were fidgeting. Lacking a strong wind to align them the yachts and cruisers faced several points of the compass; the moving tide having more influence at this time than the wind.

As he splashed happily on the smooth wet boards he also had a different view of the Bridge.

The deck and the pylons were screened by Kurraba and Kirribilli Points with their clots of apartment blocks, a smaller mishmash of styles and heights and colours, truly tacky towers from the 60s and 70s when developers made their grab for expensive harbour views, in most cases replacing large and beautiful Federation houses.

From this angle, about three-quarters end on, the famous Coathanger presented its black tracery in a more compact, steeper and more interesting curve that the flat-on tourist view. The flags on the twin poles on the top were drooping loosely. There was a little lazy movement of the blue fabric towards him, an indicator of a slight breeze from the west this early morning. He could just make out the Australian flag on the left and the state flag of New South Wales on the right. They were almost the same. They both had the red white and blue of Britain's Union Jack in the top corner. The NSW flag replaced all the white stars including those of the Southern Cross with the state's coat of arms. He knew the tradition that the senior flag is flown on the left as you enter a city and the Bridge did indeed constitute an entrance from the North.

As he often did, he allowed his eyes to slip out of focus and the crescents of girders forming the opposite sides of the distant structure slid with him. Just like those optical illusions in the books that had amused him as a kid he allowed his brain to see first from one angle, then from another as if he were a few degrees further round. First the left arch appeared closest, then the right arch.

Then back again as his brain kept changing its mind on what it was seeing. He did not control it, just let it slide. It amused him every time.

The big bonus today was the sight of a large black hulled cruise liner tied up in Circular Quay. One of the Queens perhaps? Elizabeth, Victoria or Mary? No, couldn't be. Those girls don't fit in there. Of the dozens of cruise ships that visit Sydney over the summer season three or four are too large for the Overseas Passenger Terminal. Some just squeeze under the Bridge at low tide to tie up at Barangaroo. The really big ones have to dock at Garden Island with the kind permission of the Navy.

"I'd love to get on board one of those ladies." he said out loud, arching his head back to let the cool water spray over his face.

A giggle beside him brought him back. The two ladies from the pool had climbed up the steps and stood waiting for the shower.

Shaking to clear his eyes, he thought of explaining but the women were smiling uncritically. They were both in their late forties he guessed, the shorter one dark, the taller one blonde. Both, he thought, were quite good looking and, well, quite well figured in their one piece costumes. A little too old for bikinis but not so old that they weren't both worth a look. The taller one was in fact very handsome and her smile he thought was not just forgiving but even amused and perhaps inviting.

He stepped from the shower and with a sweep of his arm invited them to take it.

The dark one stepped in and he found himself sweeping water off his limbs in conversation with the taller one.

"Nice in today."

"Yes."

"Are you a regular?"

"Well we usually come here later in the afternoon, but we thought we'd give the morning a shot. Start a little earlier..."

"Best time of day..."

"Yes, and this morning we're not it a hurry. Today I'm celebrating my divorce. After we finish our swim I'm having a glass of bubbles up on the grass with my oldest friend here."

"Really?"

Somewhere above them a small green person fluttered gracefully under a leafy branch and silently gripped the smooth pink bark of a Sydney Red Gum.

A perfect morning indeed, full of promise.

Gerry worked his way under cover of a leafy fringe. He had not seen any birds as he was coming in to land but this is unknown territory. Almost immediately he heard the gentle warble of some magpies a few trees up the path soon covered by the staccato chatter of some Noisy Miners attacking something. They were bad tempered little creatures. You'd think they owned the place. Always picking on other birds no matter how large if they dared to come anywhere nearby when the Miners had their young still under supervision.

A flash of brilliant colour above him and some more high-pitched screechings announced the arrival of a bunch of Rainbow Lorikeets. Like the motorbike gang of the skies, they were swooping and wheeling in a noisy pack, ostentatious and fearless. They flashed into the canopy of another tree out of Gerry's sight. Finding some blossoms or fruit in this tree they soon settled into contented feeding, giving out an occasional chirrup that meant they were just staying in touch with each other. They could be happy for several minutes, their red, yellow, blue and green weaving amongst the petals. Then, as though they were simultaneously struck by the dreadful thought of growing old and respectable in one place, they would all shriek off into the blue to find a more exciting venue.

'I think some quite observation is my first priority' thought Gerry slowly turning his body to see all around. Down below in the Pool looks safe if a little exposed. No birds down there, not even seagulls. Just humans chatting.

Another flash caught his eye. This time a turning of pure white mercifully high above him. It emitted a screech that redefined 'raucous', a noise that far exceeded anything the other birds could vocalise.

That is a Sulphur Crested Cockatoo, surely one of the most intimidating birds in this town. Gerry had no idea what their preferred food was. Anything it wants, I suppose.

To top it off there was a forlorn 'aaaark' drifting and floating in the air even further away. That, thought Gerry, is a crow. The Australian Raven. Glossy black. Huge. You do *not* want to meet one of them, the city cicadas had told him. He backed further under the leaves.

'This is Big Beak Central, what have I got myself into?'

A little suck of sap always helps. The *angophora costata* was not his favourite but it was OK in the circumstances. He was working his way up towards a thinner branch amongst the leaves when he heard a sound not far away. Very close in fact, in this same tree. The sound of a cicada starting up its song.

'That's brave' thought Gerry 'with all this birdlife around.'

He could not locate the source at first. He wasn't sure what he was looking for. Truth is he had never heard a song quite like it. Definitely from a medium sized cicada, but not quite as high pitched as his. Not the deeper rumble of the big blokes either. More vibrant and elegant. As it lifted in volume Gerry kept his own tympana open to listen for any tell tale clues in the other noises. Unusual in a cicada, Gerry's sound receptors were so sensitive he could pick up changes in the sounds that surrounded him, including any variation in the bird noises. Listening hard he could detect nothing new in the cockie's screech. It remained up high. The fearsome white bird with the bright yellow comb was not coming closer to check out the strange song. The freewheeling lorikeets were still intent on nibbling the nectar from their blossoms, chatting contentedly. The noisy miners were still having a spat at some other birds. Gerry judged they were not coming closer. And above it all the mournful call of the crow still circled and showed no sign of change. Relieved, Gerry forgot about the birdlife for a minute and concentrated on the cicada sound nearby. It was eerie. As a fine singer himself, he was an appreciator of the instruments of others. Unlike most of his male friends who had little ability to detect changes in pitch, and often could not hear the songs of cicadas other than their own species, Gerry had command of quite a full range of notes both when he was singing and listening. Like his female friends he also had good directional sensitivity. Females need this of course to be able to locate and move towards the calling males, for that is all that nature intended a cicada's song for. Most males simply stay in one place singing at the top of their voices, perhaps only aware of the sound of the male next to them, waiting for the ladies do all the seeking and approaching.

Gerry was more in touch with his feminine side.

That was something Merac knew. In all his years of study he had never known a cicada with Gerry's skills.

Every day of observation knowing they were finite in number he was astonished at each new revelation of Gerry's character. He was apprehensive at his young friend's boldness but he was delighted at his adventures, like when he told him about the first meeting with Monty. Every day it seemed Gerry was back with a new story. Merac was so tickled when

Gerry related the one about the paper ball in the Hyde Park bin that he wanted to rush out and buy himself a lottery ticket. How good was that!

He loved his enquiring mind, his interest in a much wider world than any cicada had a right to. He marvelled at his easy interaction with all the other cicadas as well as humans, animals and yes inanimate objects. He was guileless and innocent as all cicadas are but he seemed to have an inner strength and resolve. A desire to take on and complete a task. Gerry knew he was small to the point of insignificance but he really felt he could make a difference in the world and had quickly cottoned on to what was needed from him as Merac explained his hopes for the Quest.

If this little chap believes then we can *all* believe. He could not wait to tell Cir Franklin that they had their man.

Merac absolutely believed Cir Franklins Jewelled Quest would be an impossible dream if this little chap had not come along in this particular summer.

In a tree above McCallum Pool their champion was working his little legs silently down the branch towards the strange sound. Now was the time to find out if their confidence was correctly placed. Now was the time for Gerry to do his stuff.

With a couple of changes of position he tracked it down. There he was. Not only had he never heard the song before, he had never seen a cicada like it. Gerry had the advantage of height and could clearly see him on a branch below. The noisemaker was dark; black in fact but not a Black Prince or a Cherry Nose or a Red Eye ... compact and mysterious, quite slender but confident looking ... a dark stranger.

'Should I give a quick burst of song?' wondered Gerry 'Or flutter to attract his attention, or walk down slowly and introduce myself?'

He decided to walk.

This could take a few minutes, down the topside of one branch, a few steps down the main trunk, then out on the stranger's branch. 'I might just give a little chirrup when I reach there...' thought Gerry 'so as not to scare him.'

As he set off down the smooth branch he noticed the angophora's skin was less pink than earlier in the season when it had freshly shed its bark. The lovely pinkish orange was now fading to a grey, until next year when it would shed again and the sap would also taste fresher. He was musing on this when a rush of wings from the side half scared him to death.

'This is it!' he thought. 'I should've looked up. Should've gone down the underside of the branch. Too late!'

But the wings passed beneath him.

And didn't appear out the other side of the branch he was on.

The singing has stopped.

'It's got the dark stranger! I thought he was being too bold singing away like that in this bird-infested territory. Now he's gone! I'll never meet him. Now I'll never know his story.'

Gerry eased around the branch so he could see to the branch below.

The cicada was still there.

So was the bird.

A fierce looking bird, sleek and mature in glossy black, had its vicious hooked beak and gleaming yellow eyes just millimetres from the dark stranger.

As far as Gerry could tell they were talking.

He was flabbergasted.

'I've never heard of that before. Should I be surprised? After all, I talk to others cicadas. I talk to a human. I talk to a cat. But what kind of cicada talks to a bird! A known killer! Is this a good or a bad thing? A friendly conversation or something more sinister?'

As Gerry stared breathlessly he edged as far back as he could and still maintain vision of the pair of conspirators. He wondered for a moment if he was looking at a crow or a currawong. He thought such a dangerous looking creature had to be a crow, but it moved its position slightly and he could see the mere hint of white feathertips on the tail. No crow has that. It must be a currawong. Whatever other random white markings a currawong might have on the rest of its black body or wings it always had an arc of white across its rump and again at the tip of its tail feathers. If this was indeed a currawong it was the blackest one known to man or cicada.

Suddenly this sunny spot, which Gerry had happily embraced after his harbour crossing, which was so obviously an idyllic place for resident humans and birds – and a single strange cicada - was becoming a creepy hostile place for an outsider like himself.

This must be what quests are all about.

His brain was racing and something told him to be cautious. He moved slowly back to the topside of his branch, unable to hear the two conspirators below, knowing he could learn nothing more from his present position, and feeling much more comfortable out of the range of their glittery eyes. He felt very vulnerable on this bare branch. He'd really like to know if he had been seen.

Was a beaked death creeping up on him from below?

Then the currawong took off noiselessly, gliding down before he needed a few powerful flaps to lift himself through the lower branches and back along the Point.

Gerry's mind was now full of murky undertones. His mission had seemed so simple. Cir Franklin and Gwynneth had heard stories of a name on a bronze plaque in the vicinity of this Pool which they had not seen. Through the chain of messages that cicadas pass on from group to group, from tree to tree, across great swathes of bushland, they had learned there was a name associated with singing, and this they believed could be the clue to the correct note of the Supreme Song, the song that would charm the inanimate objects. The song that would play its part in bringing some harmony to daily life, blow away some of the cussedness, bring about some co-operation and sharing. A noble Quest and a possible one for a brave and well-meaning creature. Gerry pondered his options. He was here now. The pool and its plaque were somewhere below him. He must continue.

The Dark Cicada resumed his dark song.

Chapter Twenty One

The great gates of the Botanic Gardens were in their sights.

They had weaved their way past the fragrant garden and across the park below St Mary's Cathedral that had brought them up the slopes to Art Gallery Road and the grassy flat lands of the Domain guarded by the deep green bulk of the Port Jackson figs. Turning right, away from the group of historic buildings that faced Macquarie Street, their rear elevations an unremarkable jumble contrasting with the stately show they presented on the main road, Dad and Mum walked carrying the supplies for the day out; picnic food and drink, sunscreen and hats, a kite, a frisbie, a paper that Dad would get to read most of and a book for Mum who hopefully would manage a chapter or two.

Ellie and Tim ran and dodged, expending the first of their vast reserves of energy Mum hoped would be considerably depleted by the time they arrived home in the evening.

It was a beautiful day.

They passed the Art Gallery and Ellie pointed out to Tim the names of the famous painters and sculptors celebrated in bronze letters on the golden sandstone on the facade. She had been there on a school excursion to see the Archibald Prize winners and had asked her teacher why the men so prominently displayed on the outside walls were not the same as those whose work they had been looking at inside. Not using exactly those words of course but she had made her point. Robust discussion followed as the teacher had said: "Good question, Ellie. Anyone want to answer that?"

The best answer was from little Johnny who was never stuck for something to say. "You only make it to the outside when you are old and dead."

Fair enough. Certainly true of Raphael, Tintoretto and Donatello. None of them had entered the Archibald Prize though the kids knew some of them came back in a later life as Ninja Turtles.

The family entered the Gardens through the main gate, classically wrought in iron on sandstone columns. From there they took a weave through familiar pathways and some old favourites. This was a very busy part of the gardens. Towers of greenery dwarfed the narrow asphalt paths. Smaller exotic plants waited at the edge as if to be patted. Voices rose and fell through the twists and turns. The four of them pushing and pulling forwards and back like a box of freshly released puppies passed densely stocked beds with small black on white signs identifying species that would never be side by side in the outside world. Tim ignored the common and botanical names but seized on the country of origin and called out each one. Very occasionally Ellie was able to say where that country was in relation to other countries. Sometimes Mum chimed in to help her.

A visit to the Wollemi Pine was a must.

"How old is it?" asked Tim as he always did.

"Two hundred million years!" said Ellie confidently, more or less confirmed by Mum.

"Well this one here is not millions of years old, but it comes directly from trees that were around when the dinosaurs were here. A single old tree was discovered in a national park only about fifteen years ago. They took seeds or cuttings to produce new ones."

"I think it's a really handsome tree. Wish we could afford one." said Dad. "A mate of mine bought one when they were released and it's doing well. Still only a metre tall in a pot. He uses it as a Christmas tree."

"Why don't we go to that park and get one?" asked Tim.

"Firstly that would be illegal as they are a very rare and protected species" said Mum.

"And secondly, you wouldn't find it. No one knows exactly where they are. They've kept it all a secret so people like you can't pinch them" said Dad scooping Tim up in his arms.

"How about the Wishing Tree?" asked Mum taking Ellie's hand.

They went to the Tree and wished. Tim insisted on walking around it three times forward and three times backward. He had backed and bumped into some Asian visitors, apologised profusely and forgotten his wish by the time he finished. Ellie simply stepped forward and touched wood. Tim was persuaded to use the simpler method when he had recovered his memory.

"It works just as well." said Dad. "It's the tree that does the work, not the walking."

Moving out into more open space Tim led them accurately along the criss-crossing paths to his next favourite.

'A Very Special Tree'

"It's still dead." he said with visible disappointment as they came around the last corner of foliage.

Mum gave him a hug, as she always did.

"Maybe someday we'll come here and it will have some green tips."

Dad looked up at the grey giant. He searched each branch for signs of life.

"I spoke to one of the blokes last time and he said there was still an outside chance it would come good."

They read the sign again.

'A Forest Red Gum, home to native bees, possums and cicadas. We are keeping it because it is native to this site and it is believed to be one of the oldest trees here.'

"The bloke said they call it 'the supermarket tree' after the aborigines described all the things it provided them. Honey for drinking, bark for wrapping, resident animals for eating…"

"Gross" said Ellie.

"… wood for canoes and tools."

"Wooden tools wouldn't cut much." said Tim.

"The Aborigines managed this country very well without a Bronze Age or an Iron Age. You can achieve a lot with wooden tools."

Tim walked across the grass and stroked the great tree. His little fingers ran over the cracked bark that wrapped the base patterned like a woodsman's tilework before it gave way to smooth grey limbs lifelessly appealing to the blue sky.

Mum was sure she knew what his wish had been back at the very lively Wishing Tree.

They headed towards the water of the Harbour, the gentle curve of Farm Cove defined by a warm and weathered sandstone wall. They paused as they always did at this spot and looked down at the softly sloshing waves loosing from golden rocks light bubbles which cleared quickly in the clean water. Their ebb and flow waved the bright green seaweed one way then the other. A photo taken many summers ago of Tim on this wall sat in a silver frame in their lounge room. Mum would always remember his line that day. "The mermaid's hair is being washed."

"Right, gang. Picnic here? Or do we go round to the Chair?"

"The Chair. The Chair." Ellie danced.

"Ok we'll go. But I don't think we should eat around there. There'll be a lot of people heading that way today. So it's a brisk walk to the Chair, Ellie can be

Mrs Macquarie, then we'll come back here and as all the seats seem to be taken, we'll find a patch of grass. Is that a plan?"

"Plan."

"Plan."

"Plan."

The kids ran ahead. They knew the way.

"Have you thought more about your sister's child?"

"Yes a lot. I think I'll try finding out where she is. I know the laws on adoption have changed, the girls were talking about it the other day, and I think it is now possible to track someone down.

A birth mother finding a child is now easier and I think a child finding its birth mother is also easy. Don't know about sister of deceased mother. I'll have to check."

"Sure you want to?"

"Of course, why not? She's family. I'll give it a go."

Halfway round to the point, they had to move off the path beside the seawall as some workmen were repairing the stonework. They were separated from passersby by some orange witch's hats and a few strands of red and white plastic tape. Dad noticed that inside their workspace they had two rough piles: the stones that had been removed and some new stone which one of the men was chipping and reshaping. He loved Sydney sandstone and had spent hours looking at the many stone buildings in the city. Close up, as well as standing back across the road. As a draughtsman he could appreciate the wider view, the architect's original thoughts, the lines of the whole. He was content when he sketched them. But he was always drawn to the stone itself. The size of each block, its finish, square or carved, smooth or sparrow-picked. He checked the precision of the fitting of the joints. But most of all he loved the colours. The honey, the gold, the caramel, the sand, the beige - highlighted by summer's sun, subdued and greyed in winter.

He studied the notched edges outlining the gap in the seawall where the old stones had been removed.

That was a very pretty sketch in itself. The crisp steps of the remaining stones, weathered beige on the outside but a bright whitish yellow where protected surfaces had been freshly exposed. He made a frame with his hands and pulled it back allowing the stones to enter on each side while the centre filled with the blue/green wash of the sunlit Harbour water with one sailing boat slightly off square in a fluky breeze. A slight swivel allowed him to bring in the tip of one of the sails of the Opera House. Quintessential Sydney. 'I should sketch it one day. I should've brought my book today. I'll have to remember this picture when I get home.'

Looking at the pile of used stones stacked to one side, he wondered if the wall had been in danger of collapse. Was this structural or was this repair merely cosmetic? The stones in this pile were certainly much worn compared to the new sharp-edged golden beauties. Some he could see that had once been perfect cubes or smart rectangular solids had been scalloped and hollowed by the weather and the sea air. A couple were broken in two. One of the workmen was sorting them. He apparently thought some were reusable. Perhaps some could be recut to save a smaller but sound piece. These ones he held up for the attention of his mate with the masonry hammer and chisel who either nodded, shook his head or ... shrugged.

Fascinating, thought Dad, as the family now twenty metres away called him on.

The man sorting the old stones placed a brick-sized piece that was in his opinion no longer useful on top of the reject pile.

It seemed to jump off.

It should have done no more than slide to the bottom of the heap and come to rest but somehow halfway down it caught a corner and tripped and spun. By the time it touched the ground it had picked up momentum and tumbled end over end under the red and white tape and hit Dad just above his Chatham boatshoe on his bare ankle. Dad yelped. It bled immediately.

The workman was on his feet.

"Sorry mate. You OK? Jeez did you see that! The thing's got a mind of its own."

"It's fine. I'm fine." Dad put his fingers to the spot.

The workman offered a dirty rag.

Dad licked the blood off his fingers and pressed them again to the wound. It wasn't that bad.

By the time he'd licked his fingers again, Mum was back .

"Are you alright?"

"Yes. Really it's fine."

"How did it happen? Were you in there?" Mum pointed inside the tape as she fetched a tissue from her bag.

"No the rock came after me."

"Never seen anything like it, lady. Wouldn't happen in a million years...'

"Well it happened to my husband. We could sue you."

"Yeah, we could" chimed the children.

"Hey hey it's OK. Calm down. No-one's suing anyone. It was an accident and I'm fine. Don't worry mate we don't even have a lawyer."

"Thanks mate. Do you want to speak to my boss?"

"No. We're off. C'mon kids."

The family continued around the path with the harbour on their left to the end of the Point and Mrs Macquarie's Chair.

"That's still bleeding. Here let me look at it. I think we should take this further. They should be more careful in a public place."

"It wasn't his fault. It was the rock."

"What do you mean!"

"Oh nothing. I just had a thought when the rock bounced towards me."

"That man *threw* it at you?"

"He didn't. That rock was just having a bad day, like Tim's toast and my toothbrush the other morning. It was just after some attention."

"Your toothbrush? What *are* you talking about?"

"Sometimes things just ... happen. Things ... just do."

Mum was used to Dad's fanciful thoughts. She knew not to get exasperated or even pursue an explanation if it wasn't obvious. She tolerated most of his jokes. Indeed some of them were very funny and kept her day moving along. Some were dreadful puns, but that never stopped him. He'd face her downturned lips with his regular saying: "At least with a pun nobody gets hurt."

After one of his better plays on words she'd say you should write a book and Tim would say yes Dad a book. Tim loved Dad's jokes. Ellie usually groaned. But she had secretly told Mum many times that she thought her Dad was very clever and that she loved him for it.

They walked on laughing. Tim nudged Ellie as Mum took Dad's hand.

Mrs Macquarie's Chair was carved in 1810. It is a simple bench about 3 metres long chiselled by convicts into a low sandstone cliff. Major-General Lachlan Macquarie was the sixth Governor of the young colony, from 1810 to 1821, and regarded as one of the finest, credited with turning a ragbag penal dump into a worthy settlement from which a nation could grow. Mrs Macquarie's Road which, as an inscription notes, ran 3 miles and 377 yards from the Governor's house was designed and built at the suggestion of his wife Elizabeth, and completed in 1816 so she could stroll and take in the view. Who knows what her thoughts were when she sighted ships sailing towards her from her home far away in England? What did she think when they sailed away?

Today the Chair is still a perfect vantage point for enjoying the Harbour, the panorama is very different today but still charming. You feel you could almost reach out and touch Fort Denison.

The family found a group of school students half attending to what their teacher was saying.

Some watched as she pointed out the inscription on the rock. Some like thousands before them took in the view.

"The whole of the Sydney basin for a hundred kilometres is sitting on this kind of rock. It's called Hawkesbury sandstone. Triassic period. It's never far below the surface, you can see it sticking up in places all around the suburbs. This means very shallow and poor topsoil, which is why the early farmers had to explore west over the Blue Mountains to find good agricultural land. This sandstone is an excellent building material and the early settlers were happy to use it instead of timber. It was also used as ballast in the early sailing ships."

The teacher pointed over their heads.

"You can't quite see it from here but behind the Bridge over there is Ballast Point, where they quarried for stone to put in the ships and they also used to dump stone back there when they were finished with it. Not all of the stone was good enough for those fine buildings we looked at earlier on Macquarie Street. Some has layers of ironstone running through in. See these dark streaks and ragged edges here?"

History class or geology class, Dad wondered.

"*Not good enough.*" he thought." That's it. That's why it doesn't fit in. It's a ballast rock not a wall rock."

"What are you mumbling about? Why are you smiling?"

When the class had moved on, when the crowds had thinned and some cicadas were starting up in the trees near the end of the Point, they let Ellie take her turn on the bench.

"I am master of all I survey."

"Mistress."

"Boss. And as your boss I decree we go back and eat."

On the way back Dad stopped at the worksite.

"Back again for more? How's the leg?"

Dad pointed to the piece of rock that hit him. "Was this piece in the wall you just knocked down?"

"Yep. Wrong place wrong time we reckon. A bit of rogue rock. It's not going back in ... too hard to chip. See that red streak. Got a bit of ironstone through it. Dunno why they used it in the first place."

"Is that your blood on it, Dad?"

"No son, that's what makes that little fella different. Could I have this rock?" Dad asked.

"Go for your life, mate. If you want to carry the bastard. I woulda just chucked it in the Harbour but the boss calls this an important conservation job and we're on our best behaviour because we have a bit of an audience."

He did an exaggerated bow to an elderly lady who had stopped to examine their work.

Dad picked up the rock and weighed it in his hand as he walked away.

"I know what this little fella would like. I have an idea."

"Your father had gone mad. Don't get too close to him."

They found a spot and spread out their rug and their picnic food. The rock sat on the grass beside Dad, just off the rug. He ignored it while they ate and drank. Mum thought it was all too silly but the kids kept it in mind. Ellie poked her tongue out at it but Tim seemed to pick up something from his Dad and gave their mute lunch companion a small smile and an occasional wave.

"We'll walk along the water to the Quay and then back home. Everyone OK with that?"

Everyone was fine with that. It was still a lovely day with plenty of time.

"Can we get a drink at the Opera House?"

"Sure. I just have something to do with my rock and a ferry first."

They walked along the seawall of Farm Cove through the lower levels of the Botanic Gardens, across the forecourt of the spectacular bulk of the Opera House with only a nod of familiarity. They did this walk often, passing groups and pairs of tourists with open mouths and shutters.

Arriving at the next seawall overlooking the merry dance of ferries in an enclosed horseshoe of water, they ambled around the Writers Walk, a series of bronze plaques the size of large pizzas set in the pavement, which quoted from writers of the last two hundred years, visitors and residents, who had something to say about Sydney and its Harbour.

Dad pointed out one of the smaller cream and green ferries with the twin hulls.

"See that one there, the Borrowdale, it's named after one of the ships of the First Fleet. And that one coming in, the Alexander. And over there, the Sirius. There were nine of them, I think."

"Can you name them all, Dad?"

"Sorry, darling, we can look it up if you're interested."

At the wharves, Dad found the ferry he was looking for.

And so it was that the rock which had never wanted to be fixed in a wall was hidden in the anchor chain of the Lady Northcott, a Lady Class ferry which was used mainly on the route from Circular Quay to Taronga Zoo. The red streaked piece of ancient sandstone had indeed been a piece of ballast in a couple of His and then Her Majesty's sailing ships for a large part of the nineteenth century. It had become accustomed to the pull and surge of the ocean. The slap and hiss of deep water. The creaking of close-by timbers and of hemp ropes high above. It had tolerated the brief stopovers in busy harbours while the ship was loaded but it revelled again and again in the tumble of the wild seas. It had travelled hundreds of thousands of miles before the decommissioning of its last vessel had seen it dumped on the edge of the Harbour and finally collected and imprisoned in that wretched wall.

Now Dad had given it a second surge of life.

As the harbour ferries never use their anchors, the rock remained undiscovered for almost five years covering several thousand more miles on the mostly tranquil waters of the Harbour. But it can be said that it had the time of its life.

Sometimes in summer when it came past Farm Cove snug in its rusty links it could hear the cicadas singing.

Chapter Twenty Two

Gerry restarted his slow crawl down the branch to the main trunk.

His little heart thumped.

'It's OK to be scared' he told himself, 'I just have to keep moving.'

As much as he was wary, he was curious.

He was intrigued to know the background of a cicada he'd never seen or heard before; he hoped there was a really good story there which he could proudly pass on to Merac; but finding out more might mean his life and his mission being terminated very rapidly, unless there was a less sinister explanation for the meeting he'd just witnessed with the currawong.

Has this Dark Cicada done some deal with the local birds?

What price do you pay for that? Can you sell your soul to a mortal enemy?

As he approached the junction he traversed to have a look over the edge. The Dark Cicada hadn't moved. He would be facing away when Gerry reached his branch. Gerry moved out of sight again and down the main trunk. He swung around it and up under the branch which carried the stranger. His little claws dug softly into the smooth bark just enough to take his weight. He moved slowly towards the top of the branch.

As he cleared the outside circumference, the Dark Cicada was waiting, staring down at him.

"We were expecting you."

"We?" Gerry struggled to see who else was there. There was no-one else on the branch.

"The birds and I. You are the Green Traveller, are you not?"

"I've never been called that before."

"Perhaps that was the code that was passed on. What is your name?"

"Gerry."

"Pleased to meet you. My name is Max."

He seemed genuinely friendly although his aura of mystery persisted. It was an air of superiority and formality Gerry was unused to. All the cicadas he knew were correct and well mannered but they were all on the same social standing and treated each other with an open informality. Even Cir Franklin, although he was a tad pompous, allowed everybody to be equal.

"I am here to help you find the name you are looking for."

"Am I looking for a name?"

"That's what was sung on to me. A name and a note. Correct?"

It was against his nature but Gerry still didn't trust this dark stranger.

Gerry heard the thump of heavy wings behind him. Of course he could not turn so he waited for the blow. He could hear the scrabble of large claws on bark as the bird settled on the branch behind him.

"This is my friend Gerry." said the Dark Cicada looking past.

Gerry executed a quick flutter turn and saw the biggest bird he had ever seen in his life, so close he had to lower his back legs and raise his front to allow his gaze to travel up. The huge black beak, lowered to rest on the branch, had random white scratches and a wicked point. It thickened, solid as a steel pipe, as it became part of a head the size of a grapefruit. Brown feathers flecked with white swept tightly up as though brushed back over a full brow. The eyes were dark brown, big deep pools of mystery. Gerry could feel his life being examined.

No-one moved for a full five seconds.

"Hello Gerry." said the Kookaburra at last.

The face that filled his vision was as impassive as a feathered Sphinx, although with a much more generous beak, but could Gerry see a smile in those deep brown eyes?

"I've heard you like lizards and snails. And you don't like cicadas. Is that correct?"

"Correct." The deep voice crackled.

"And you're not thinking of going on a cicada diet anytime soon?"

"Don't make me laugh' said the Kookaburra.

"No don't do that." said Max. "His laugh is very loud."

The Kookaburra is also known locally at the Laughing Jackass, so named by the early settlers because of its song, the like of which they had never heard from any European bird. It sounded to them like a hysterically braying donkey. These are very handsome birds, the largest of the Kingfisher family, white chested with brown back and wings, with delicate soft blue dabs patterning their wingfeathers. Just one of them, starting with a deep throaty *kook, kook, kook, kook* (yes, that's why they have the

Aboriginal name of kookaburra) builds up to an astonishing cackle of prolonged laughter which rings through native bushland and also through town and suburb all up the east coast of Australia.

Three or four of them laughing together, which is not uncommon because they do live in extended families, can be deafening. A popular Aussie childrens' song has it that kookaburras laugh when it's going to rain.

"Why aren't they eating us?" Gerry asked Max.

"These are all local birds, and this is a very civilised peninsula. The territorial boundaries are ancient and well respected by all the different kinds of birds. All the nests in the hollow trees have been allocated for years. They normally have no problems chasing cicadas but a couple of days ago when I arrived they heard me sing for the first time. Of course they have never heard anything like it, and as you know many birds are great appreciators of others' music, so being quite well fed and not desperate to eat me they called a truce for a minute to check things out. A currawong approached me and said they were curious about my song."

"I'm curious too. You said you'd just arrived. You're not from around here?"

"No, I'm from Avoca."

Gerry had heard that name before somewhere. But not in relation to cicadas, he thought.

"It's a long way north of here. On the coast. It has a beautiful beach, I've been told."

"Did you fly?"

"No I came in a car."

"You can drive?"

The Kookaburra started: *kook kook kook kook*

"No please. It's not that funny."

"Sorry" said Gerry.

"I've linked up with a family who has a house up there on the beach. They also have a house along this Point. I hitched a lift down when I heard you were to be here."

"How did you do that?"

"Climbed onto one of the kid's backpacks just before they were getting into the car. It's easy to work with humans once you get over the initial fear."

"I know. Why are you here for me?"

"You'll have to ask the Wizard that."

"The Wizard?"

"Your friend."

"Merac?"

"Is that his name? We just heard the Wizard and the Green Traveller wanted some help."

"So you don't know why you're here?"

Max cleared his throat. Gerry picked up something in his speaking voice that he'd picked up in the song he'd heard earlier. He was smaller than Gerry, much finer in silhouette but his speech had a rich timbre, a note that Gerry had not heard before in any of the city cicadas.

"It appears I am rather special. My species that is. Our family name is, are you ready for this, *Cicadetta hunterorum Moulds.* We only come from one place in Avoca. Just one street really. We inhabit just a few big trees in one park which fortunately has been spared development. There's no serious paving, just a few pathways. So every summer a small group of us emerge. There were not that many of us last year and we may not be long for this world. But when the word was sung around that the Wizard was seeking a unique song, they don't come much more unique than us. Our song is what he's after. He wants to use it, not for humans, but for those other things ... those objects."

"I know them. He and our leader Cir Franklin have a Quest, a mission, to try and make humans a little more happy by making the inanimate objects a little more happy."

"And you fit in, where?"

"I'm to find a name and a note."

"The name you are looking for should be on that plaque down there. On one of those two plaques set in the rock near the entrance to the pool. I have already had a look at them. You may know what you are looking for when you read them."

"Would the note be the one you've been singing?"

"Could be. Want to try it?"

"Sure."

"We don't have to worry about the birds. And you won't be troubled by any females flying up. There are no females within a hundred kilometres who would be interested in this song."

The Dark Cicada cleared his tymbals and sang.

Gerry started up beside him, using his pitch control to drop his natural song down to the level of his companion.

"Still too high" said Max.

Gerry dropped his pitch. Not quite right. He dropped it again. Very close but still just off. If you put two vibrations together with frequencies that are close but not perfect it really jars the ears. The clashing notes offended him but he knew he was almost there.

He slid down again, easing on to it...

Suddenly the two sets of tiny drummers were in perfect synchronisation. Feeling their songs come together like two matching graphs overlapping they raised the decibels. Now they were two musicians on stage immersed in their perfect performance; they kept their eyes on each other and pushed it as hard as they could. At way over 120 decibels the din pierced their corner of the world.

From the next tree a couple of birds shrieked and took flight.

On the grass below them a glass tinkled as it shattered.

Lowering the volume slightly as a prelude to a quick cut off, Gerry looked with new eyes at the Dark Cicada in the silence.

"Masterful" he said.

"You can join the Avoca singers any day." replied Max.

"That was really fun."

"Certainly was, but we do have some work to do. Let's find the names you're looking for."

Set into the rock wall above the steps leading down to the pool are two plaques side by side. One is quite large in black marble with recessed lettering engraved in the manner of a memorial stone from the 1930s. The other is much smaller, a bronze casting with raised letters. Max and Gerry fluttered down to sit on the facing fence where they had a good view.

In the morning light with the sun still below the buildings and trees behind it, the older plaque was difficult to read but keen eyes soon had it scanned.

MUNICIPALITY OF NORTH SYDNEY
THE MACCALLUM POOL
THIS TABLET COMMEMORATES THE SEVICES
RENDERED TO THE RESIDENTS BY
HUGH MACCALLUM ESQ
IN CONNECTION WITH THIS SWIMMING POOL
UNVEILED ON 29TH APRIL 1933 BY
ALD RL HODGSON MAYOR

"Does that help" asked Max "is that what you are looking for?"

Gerry was not at all sure.

"Mr MacCallum sounds like a fine gentleman, but I can't see anything there that leads to a song."

"What about the other one?"

The small bronze said clearly and boldly:

NORTH SYDNEY MUNICIPALITY
THIS POOL
WAS EXTENSIVELY RENOVATED 53 YEARS
AFTER ITS ORIGINAL CONSTRUCTION
& OFFICIALLY RE-OPENED BY
MRS JOAN A. SUTHERLAND
A LIFETIME RESIDENT OF
CREMORNE POINT.
ON 15TH DECEMBER, 1985.
R.D. KEMPSHALL   TOWN CLERK

"Pity the Mayor couldn't make it."

"Obviously not a keen swimmer."

"Could Mr Kempshall be the name we want?"

"Doesn't ring any bells for me. But that other name ..."

"Mrs Sutherland?"

"Yes, Joan. I have heard the Botanic Gardens cicadas talk about her. They know her as a singer.

They have enormous respect for her. I think she had something to do with the Opera House. I don't know if she's still there, her story could be passed down."

"Sounds promising. So you'll take that name back to the Magician?"

"I will. He'll know what to make of it. Joan Sutherland. I have a good feeling about her."

"Make sure you get it back there."

"Easy peasy. If I've crossed the Harbour once I can do it again. I can see the Opera House from here."

"Why not take it easy. Why don't you rest up tonight?"

Even though he'd done his longest journey in a car, the Dark Cicada had a very good idea of the distance a normal cicada could fly. He could barely make it across his park in Avoca, and the Opera House, clear as it appeared across the water, was a long way further than he'd ever flown.

But Gerry was excited and determined.

"No, Merac will be waiting. I have to keep to the plan. We agreed on the early morning flight over here with the return flight in the afternoon. He'll be expecting me this evening. And he'll be eager for the information. I get the feeling it's really important for him, not just for Cir Franklin's Quest. I just have one niggling thought. Why do you suppose I had to come over here for that name? Wouldn't it be ... couldn't we have found it somewhere else? Why couldn't Merac have come over here?"

"Maybe you could have found that name. But the Magician couldn't have found me. Or my song. I'm sure he knew that."

"He does know a lot."

"Who knows how these things go. With so many of us in song each year, it's hard to tell. There is so much information being sung around, it's impossible to know what's news and what is remembered from before. This has been a very busy peninsula for cicadas for generations. The songs ring all the way round the city and countryside. Every tree in summer is full of tymbals singing the words around and tympana taking them in. Which cicada first read these plaques and which one made the connection to your Quest? How did the city cicadas know about me? How did they find me and bring me down to you? Why is my song so important? Your Magician obviously thinks it is."

"He said I would hear a song on my Quest. I think it must be yours. It's the pitch of your song that's important. It's different to anything I've heard."

"Something to be said for being from a small family."

"I had a thought. Do you think that everything that has been sung before is now a part of us all?"
"Hmmm. Not too sure about that. Then again, perhaps that's right. Now I think about it, yes ..."

"Merac says you can't create or destroy matter. Every atom that every existed is still here, just in a different form."

"But we know that thoughts and memories *can* be created. So you're saying that once they are, they never go away as long as those who hear them still remember and talk about them and pass them on."

"I'll discuss that with Merac; if we come up with anything new, we'll sing it up to you. What will you do now?"

"Maybe chat to a few birds for a while. It's going to be a nice warm day. I'll have a bit of a sing even though there are no girls to hear me. The family will be going back up to Avoca this weekend and I'll get myself in the car somehow. I'll be home in plenty of time."

"Plenty of time for what?"

"To hear all about your success. All the cicadas will know. They'll sing the word through."

Gerry looked at Max head on. Their jewels sparkled.

"Time to go."

"Yes. Time to go. Thankyou."

"Thank you. You're the one on the mission. You'll be safe to take off from here any time, but once you are over that water you're on your own. I can take care of the birds. I can do nothing with the waves. Cicadas and water don't mix."

"I'll stay dry. Keep Singing."

Gerry launched himself and was immediately lifted by a sharp updraft in the freshening wind. Attempting a farewell wave with his wings, he abruptly dropped several metres closer to the waves. He pulled himself up with a blur of rapid beating. It wasn't quite what he had in mind; he hoped it looked to Max like a daring display of airmanship, his own version of an Immelmann Turn.

He set his course for the opposite shore, with a name and a song fixed in his mind.

Looking ahead he could see the Opera House.

Allowing a moment of warm anticipation he could see himself safely in the city meeting room, sitting with Cir Franklin and Merac (I must tell him he's known as The Magician) with Gwynneth fussing over him. "I always knew that boy had it in him..."

He saw himself sucking on selected sap and chatting modestly to his male friends while the girls crowded at the edges, as he told the story of his successful Quest. The skimming of the Opera House sails, the turreted Fort, the boats, the waves, the trees, the birds, the pool, the plaques, the Dark Cicada, the Kookaburra, the incredible song....

Focussing again on the mission he realised that the Opera House wasn't where it should be. There it was, way off to the left of his vision. OK, he thought, assuming the Opera House isn't moving that means I am shifting quite rapidly to the right.

He looked below and saw two boys in a sailing dingy set with a bursting spinnaker charging into Shell Cove where the boats were all now tautly aligned, trembling as they pulled at their bowlines, pointing into the stiffening Southerly.

"Uh oh."

A gentle breeze riffling the leaves of a tree as you are coming in to land is a daily cicada challenge. Mostly a pleasurable one, asking of you: how cleanly can you dodge and land? There is not much downside, you could collect a faceful of greenery or a flick from a swinging twig, at worst you'd have to go around and have another crack at it. Barring a Beak Encounter you always make the trunk in the end.

But out here over the Harbour a wind that can shift a volume of air as large as a stadium 100 metres in a few seconds, is just way too big for a tiny flying machine to cope with, struggling as hard as it might within that volume.

Gerry knew he was in trouble. Committed to the flight, already well out over the water, he knew he could never make the far shore, not even half way to Fort Denison which he could see through blurring vision now way off to his left.

He would turn back. Max would understand.

Would Max still be there? Had he gone to rejoin his family? What about all those birds? Would he still have immunity without Max's presence? Without the Dark Cicada, Gerry was just another greengrocer; another thoughtless meal.

In his peripheral vision he could tell he was already far north of his start point. Against this wind, now with a gusting angle of easterly in it, he could not even make it back to the Pool.

Who knew what terrors could be waiting in the greenery if he landed further up the Point?

Below him the moored yachts had their noses up sniffing desperately to leap into the action they were built for, timbers creaked and rigging lines twanged as he was pushed further up the Cove. Helpless, he crossed the far shore of the narrow wedge of water with a speed that scared him as he headed towards houses and apartments. He saw warm red tiles topping off the older houses and grey patches of concrete on the roof gardens of the newer waterfront constructions.

Some of the sting went out of the wind and he dropped to the comparative safety of messy swirls and eddies around these dwellings and the trees that separated them. The peninsula he was now crossing was itself not very wide and even at the modest height he had descended to he could see himself being swept right across it over to another larger body of water. This part of the Harbour has a very busy shoreline. It was time to get down and reassess. He looked for the thickest patch of trees, and saw some surrounding a small house with a lawn.

Almost in control again he scooted over a narrow road, past the maroon painted doors of a street frontage garage and headed for a tall eucalypt on the edge of the grass. In its lee the air was hardly moving and he flickered past several groups of people walking up a brick path and turned on the wingpower to bring himself to the safety of a smooth grey branch spouting sturdily from the main trunk.

"Did you see that?" said a young girl whose hair he had almost brushed.

"What's that darling?" said her grandmother.

"A cicada. It's up there. I wonder if it's the one May Gibbs writes about."

"I don't think so darling."

The girl opened the book she was holding and found the words she was looking for amongst the lovely drawings of the gumnut babies.

"It could be. Listen Gran, I've just been reading about them. Here, look. *'The Journey Begins'*

One very hot night when the cicadas were singing so loudly that Snugglepot couldn't hear his father snoring, he and Cuddlepie crept out of bed and out of the house.' See, cicadas, I was right! I think that's one of them up there."

May Gibbs? Snugglepot? Cuddlepie?

Gerry kept very quiet. It was hours before his heart returned to normal.

He moved around the branch. It was late afternoon. Below him people were moving towards the garage and out into the street.

What kind of place is this, he wondered. I'll have a good look around in the morning.

He settled himself under a spray of leaves in the softly moving breeze and prepared to settle down. He rested.

As night slid his light away, a quick look around his new tree showed Gerry's expert eye that this was a scribbly gum. On the bark of main trunk and lower branches were the easily recognised random squiggles, the rounded zig zags that greengrocers liked to sing along to. But Gerry was in no mood for a song.

He moved up the branch to find some thinner greener twigs. A quick sap before bedtime is always a good idea. He slid his rostrum into the soft bark and took in the sweet liquid. He liked the taste of *eucalyptus haemostoma* and sucked deeply. A few minutes later he was feeling quite refreshed, quite his inquisitive self again. He wouldn't attempt another Harbour crossing tonight although the wind seemed to be dying down. The morning he confidently predicted would be better. Meanwhile, there was just enough daylight for him to have a quick look at this house. On the lawn was a dropped brochure and he whirred down to examine it.

It read: *May Gibbs' Nutcote. Home of the Gumnut Babies.*

I could use a bit of wind right now, he thought, to blow these pages open so I can read on. He saw the words he had heard the little girl mention, *Snugglepot* and *Cuddlepie* and a drawing of two cute little babies sitting on a gumleaf. They had gumnuts for hats. There was a photo of the Harbour framed in some arches - that must be on the other side of the house. Also a web address. Not a lot of use to Gerry this far away from Merac's laptop. He scratched at the edge of the leaflet and turned the page. There was the story of the lady who lived in this house for many years, an author and illustrator who gave Australian children a fantasy land of little creatures she brought to life from the native flora she loved. He spent a few minutes reading all about her and admiring her drawings of the wide-eyed innocent gumnut babies, and their enemies the wicked banksia men. Hey, there was a kookaburra there as well. Not looking nearly as fierce as the one he had just met. He liked this lady and he read her brochure front to back.

Gerry took to the air and flew over the low roof of the house. It was quite close to the Harbour. In the distance rising solidly above a skyline of apartments on the next shore he could see the criss-cross black bulk of the arch of the Harbour Bridge. He was looking at it almost end on. He couldn't see the Opera House but it would have to be just to the left. Now he had a great fix for plotting his course for the morning.

Meanwhile he checked out the trees in this sloping garden. There was a youngish angophora off to the right and a very old banksia (is that where May saw the bad men?) and a scraggly casurina right down near the water's edge.

He turned to come back and was about to land in a Port Jackson fig near the corner of the house when he saw a scurrying movement right where he was headed. Two, no, three creatures were moving quickly up the branches towards him, bright eyes glittering above cheeky pointed snouts, sleek grey fur rippling as they scampered, long tails waving like slow snakes, balancing their movements. Those are not cats he thought. He pulled out of his dive and wheeled back towards the angophora, landing halfway up where its slender pink barked trunk forked.

By the time he'd turned around to look back, the three ringtailed possums were not where they had been. He caught sight of the tail-waving backsides of two who were heading rapidly down the lower limbs of the fig. Whoa! The biggest one had already made it to the lawn below and was scampering towards the base of the angophora.

"Who are these guys!" Gerry thought.

The big possum began to climb his tree with amazing agility and speed.

Gerry took to the air.

"Are they after me!"

He couldn't wait to find out.

Gerry didn't know a lot about possums, but he thought they only ate flowers and plants. Did I look like a floating blossom or have I just missed out on making new friends?

Whatever, it does significantly affect tonight's sleeping arrangements. I'm glad I spotted them before they found me dozing. These guys could easily roam either side of the house.

He returned across the roof to his scribbly gum flying in as high up as he could and gripping a small bunch of leaves near the end of the highest branch.

As he swung in the dying breeze in the near darkness he thought once again how hazardous life can be for a cicada out of his home tree. I supposed you can't expect everyone around you to be aware of the importance of your Quest, and spread roses in your path.

You just have to tough it out alone.

The good news is I now have a good direction for tomorrow's take-off and I'm a lot closer than I was before I started today's disastrous flight. In an emergency I can make a landing on the way. But if I know anything about wind, it will be kinder tomorrow. A good chance of a nor'easter.

The bad news is swaying around all the way up here I won't get much rest.

Chapter Twenty Three

The sun had long since flicked its first shafts at the city when Gerry settled down for a delicious, nourishing and late breakfast. He had been very tired from the previous day and he also wanted to clear his mind of some images from last night. Cicadas don't actually sleep as deeply as we humans do but they relax into a dreamy state and review their day's events until the warmth of the sun brings them fully awake again.

His mind had been filled with drawings of gumnut babies and banksia men, competing with lively images of possums and all kinds of birds. As a world to retreat into he far preferred the drawings of the landscape that May Gibbs had created. He thought it must be very satisfying to amuse and educate generations of little ones.

But as the sun climbed he knew that world was not for him today.

Still he now felt a part of her history and hoped one day his mission would be set in a song that kids would find as enjoyable and as important as her art.

Finishing with a good slurp, he was not sure whether to tell Merac that his new favourite was scribbly bark sap rather than lemon scented. Really, he'd be happy with either. Maybe one day I can try half and half. Half fill the rostrum with one; top up with other. Do a handstand. Swirl it around ...yum.

Gerry was a simple soul. Still half child, half adult. Boyish thoughts were never far from his mind, but it was time to put away childish things. Today he had to be the hero.

Before that he'd just take on a little more sap. Wait for the wind to die down. That then meant he felt like a quick nap. Soon it was lunchtime. Another snack. Another nap.

It was into the afternoon by the time he cleared himself for takeoff.

He deliberately stayed low to cross the water before he had to beat hard to rise up and make it over Kirribilli Point with its jumble of apartment blocks. A full view of the Bridge opened up for him with the Bradfield Highway curving between the pylons. On its sweeping lanes hundreds of cars glittered and cast speckled sunlight back at him. He felt strong.

But 'strong' for a cicada is a very small parcel of strength.

Today, unfortunately, the wind wasn't from the north east.

It was still from the south, very gentle but steady, and Gerry was forced to track resolutely against it. As he turned towards his goal he could feel himself losing power and losing altitude.

Once again he thought of turning back. He knew he could return to somewhere near his start point. The wind would see to that.

But there, there was the Opera House. He could almost touch it.

No turning back this time.

He beat harder. Every muscle drew every drop of energy from the sweet sap that sustained him.

No cicada had ever tried so hard.

But it wasn't enough.

The Opera House slipped from view. Looking down he could see he was not even over the safety of Kirribilli any more. He was going backwards, dropping fast towards the water.

He remembered Max's words: cicadas and water don't mix.

Not quite true. Gerry liked rainwater. All cicadas are caught in a few showers in their lives and they find it refreshing. Quite cleansing. Rain-washed air feels lovely to fly through and many remember the sound and the seeping of rain water that summoned them from their holes in the ground for their first appearance as adults on the earth.

But Gerry had never tasted salt water. Fresh clear water falling from the sky, swirling or even pooling was one thing, dark green deep water as a choppy landing strip was something else.

He hit hard.

Instead of folding his wings and trying for a belly landing he was still frantically whirring as he landed on his side. Through the shock, it felt as though he had ripped his extended flailing wing completely off his shoulder, but as he bobbed over the first waves he realised it was still attached but he could not fold it back. His two left wings, large and small, were fine but his top right wing stayed out at right angles to his body. It hurt as nothing had ever hurt him before. For a moment it distracted him from an even larger and terminal problem. He was now in the Harbour and from there could not possibly take off again.

As if the chill of the water and the sting of the salt beginning to close down his body's depleted strength was not enough Gerry the Greengrocer had to face some final brutal assaults. If he was facing one way with the waves from his left, his right wing stretching out acted like a stabiliser, keeping his head above water. But the chop and the wind were fluky. Sometimes he found himself the other way round and the slop of the waves under his wing pitched him over, under and upside down. You don't have to have almost drowned before, you don't have to have experienced near death on a previous occasion to know when your time is up. You know.

Gerry relaxed.

So it ends. I have the knowledge. It's here with me, Merac.

I tried. Please believe how hard I tried.

If only I could have sung it on. Now it sinks with me. Maybe you will find another champion. Someone who is more up to the Quest.

The last thing he saw was a flash of white. He heard sounds he'd never heard before and then the tightness in his chest. With no movement of his damaged wings he was flying.

No more effort, no more pain.

He rose up and up.

Chapter Twenty Four

The Lady Northcott thrummed through the water for several trips a day taking passengers from Circular Quay to the Zoo a few kilometres down the Harbour towards the Heads. Taronga Zoo had been a much loved fixture in the suburb of Mosman on the northern side of the Harbour for very nearly one hundred years. 21 hectares of fauna fascination for kids, parents, grandparents and serious students.

When Merac was studying in London he dropped into a conversation in his local with a group of tanned Australian men boasting to a group of pale English girls about their birthplace. One of them was explaining how the animals at the Sydney zoo had the most expensive views in the world. 'Billions of dollars of prime real estate devoted to our furry friends.' he said.

"Wait a minute" Merac had chipped in confidently. "It's not much of a view. You can't see the Harbour from there."

'Of course you can' the others had argued. Merac then in his twenties suddenly worked out he hadn't been to the Zoo since he was four or five. Although his memories of elephant rides, penguins, baboons and snoozy lions were clear enough, he hadn't realised that he would have been below fence height all the way round the many pathways past the cages and enclosures. Of course no adult had thought to pick him up just to show him the Harbour. He began to blabber out his explanation, but they shut him up and made him buy the next round.

"What do you think Taronga means in aboriginal, you dill?

"Don't know" Red faced.

"Beautiful view."

Merac had never forgotten that. Humiliated, he had even missed out on following up on one of the girls he quite fancied. Good to have youth behind you, he thought.

On the green and cream ferry this day were the usual mix of locals and tourists. A family group from America were sitting up the front, loving the swish and swirl of wind on their faces as the diesels way below them throbbed their way towards the Opera House.

One of the girls standing at the rail was watching one of the seagulls lazily following the ferry when it banked off to the side and swooped towards the water.

Normal behaviour for a seagull, she thought. Suddenly, not so normal, a very large brown and white bird flecked with blue equipped with a huge beak attacked the seagull, flapping it away from its intended prey. The gull returned once but was no match for the big bird that had begun a guttural growl as it circled so the white seabird retreated squawking and took up station nearer the stern.

The big bird took another run and scooped up something from the surface in its beak. It rose up, seemed to consider its position for a second then swooped down onto the bow-rail of the ferry.

It hopped onto the deck and carefully placed a small green parcel on the worn grey planks. Standing its ground boldly for a couple of seconds it seemed to study the humans, summing them up as turned its head to fix them with one huge brown and bright orb.

"Wow" said George Halliday of Roanoke, Virginia, standing up to be closer to his daughter.

"We didn't see one of them critters back there."

Jim Roberts of Cremorne, sitting beside the family from the USA, helped out.

"That is a kookaburra" he said, "and his dinner there *was* a cicada. A greengrocer by the look of it. Well, an ex-greengrocer. Deceased."

The Kookaburra took off.

"He didn't eat it Daddy. But he hurt it, see. Its wing is broken"

"The naughty bird killed it." said her younger sister with finality.

They all went quiet. The chug of the engines continued. A seagull mourned.

"No" the first girl squealed. "It's moving. Daddy, do something."

"Stand back, I'm a doctor" said George stepping up to the plate.

He knelt down and picked Gerry up. George was a doctor and without sons of his own he had worked for many years with local football teams as a medico. He enjoyed the masculine rough and tumble, the bit hits, the big plays, and he was also able to render assistance on the spot for injuries received.

He knew a dislocated shoulder when he saw one.

He put his glasses on and studied the cicada's anatomy, holding him in his surgeon's hands, slowly turning him watching the legs move feebly. He could see nothing actually torn or obviously broken. It seemed to be a case of overextension.

He thought 'This little fella's probably not long for this world, but we'll see what we can do.' With his thumb underneath he raised the floppy wing and rotated it gently. He was able to fold it back. It seemed without damage.

George held the cicada up in his hand and turned it around. It now appeared neat and symmetrical, and was standing squarely on its feet. George could feel the tiny claws tickling his palm as Gerry moved gingerly forward.

"Cute little fella, huh. Did you get a good look at him, girls?"
He held his hand out towards them.

"Is he alright Daddy? What a nasty bird."

"He looks better Daddy. You healed him."

"I sure hope so, although I guess we'll never know, I don't speak cicada. Well not with an Ossie accent, that's for sure."

"Daaaad."

Above them unseen the kookaburra wheeled and took off for Cremorne Point.

The Lady Northcott was now close to the Opera House, slowing down to wait for an empty berth at the wharves of the Quay. The waters were chopped by several moving watercraft, including one of the large Manly ferries. George held on as the ferry swayed.

He turned to Jim.

"So this is one of your Ossie cicadas. Great colour green. We have 13 year cicadas where I come from. They're not such a nice colour. It sure is an amazing sight when they come out. Millions of them just pop up in one day."

"Lucky your Dad was here to save this little bloke, eh girls." Jim said, having observed the miracle.

"Can we keep him Daddy?"

"No. That's not what he'd want. Once we're ashore we'll find a tree, maybe in that park over there."

Gerry was way ahead of them. His wing was indeed back where it should be; he whirred a little to make sure. Yes it was painful but definitely working. As George's hand turned he could see the Red Twins emerging from the silhouette of the mighty sails.

Suddenly he felt an unexpected glow in his jewels, a strange warmth. He wondered what was causing that. He looked around trying to locate a source. He crawled to the edge of the doctor's hand and stared down at the bow. Something was coming from there. Something he thought he should understand. All he could see was a red streaked chunk of sandstone about the size of a brick settled down almost invisibly in the rusty links of the anchor chain. A rock?

But now as the ferry moved forward again he leapt at his chance. He now knew what the Kookaburra had done for him. He knew what the man with the soft hands had done. But he was a cicada on a mission and he took to the air. Just seconds later he was over the Writers' Walk, over the afternoon crowds and up past the Opera House forecourt. He felt so exhilarated he kept going all the way into the city towards Merac's house. Nothing could stop him now.

"Well from one Aussie on behalf of another who didn't stop long enough to thank you, thank you." Jim Roberts extended his hand. George clasped it cheerfully.

"We're just loving our time here. It's been a great day for us. Not only have we saved an Ossie's life, we've been to Bondi, early this morning. We had a surf. Then we went to the zoo this afternoon. Not nearly enough time unfortunately. We'll have to come back. And this evening we're going to your Opera House here for an opera."

"Which one?"

"The Magic Flute."

"Is that the young people's version everyone's talking about?"

George's wife was now standing up.

"It sure is. The girls will love it. We missed it in the States. But not this time. We'll be there with bells on."

They slid into the wharf.

"How long do you have here?"

"We have another seven days altogether. Then back stateside. It's winter there now."

"Well I hope we keep the sunshine up for you." said Jim, feeling the southerly rising and eyeing the clouds.

The engine rumbled into reverse. The water churned. The deckhand nonchalantly lasooed the bollard. The rope squeaked as it strained to arrest the weight of the vessel. The gangway clattered out.

"Enjoy your stay." said Jim.

Faintly across the water not far from where he lived he could hear the *kookkookkooka* cry starting up. He smiled as he heard the whole family of the king of kingfishers erupting into an exultant cackle which swirled around the waters of the Harbour and tickled the darker clouds which were just beginning to drift in from the south.

It was going to rain.

Minutes later the first big spots were hitting the hot pavements, releasing the first whiffs of ozone that would cleanse the city. A few drops flew into the windows of the house with Gerry as he fluttered through. The big room was empty so he whirred up to the end where Merac was working, totally involved in his writing. The cicada settled on the end of the bench without him noticing then couldn't resist a triumphant burst of song. Not wishing to reveal his new and important songsheet just yet, he rasped out his regular frequency at a modest level which the professor recognised immediately.

"Gerry!"

"I'm home."

Looking at him Merac put his chin on his desk. Gerry walked up as fast as his little legs would move and gave him a headie. Well, more of a nosey.

"I was worried, Gerry."

"No need to be. I was fine. Easy peasy."

Gerry swaggered across to Merac's notes as though he wanted to check them.

"You're a day late. Anything happen?"

"Anything apart from the sails, the boats, the surprise fort, the lady with the scarf, the pool, the Dark Cicada, the big bad birds, the plaques, the song I think you want, the name I think you want, the wind blowing me way off course, the May Gibbs house, more wind, the dive in the harbour, the laughing kookaburra, the broken wing, the doctor who fixed me ...nothing much."

Merac laughed.

"You have to tell me everything. But we'll take it one thing at a time. You broke a wing?"

"It's OK now. I made it here on all four. Should I start at the beginning?"

"Someday when we have time to settle down you can tell me every little thing. But Cir Franklin should be here soon and I know what *he* will want. It might be better if you give it all to me first. Start with the important parts of the Quest. Did you find what we need?"

"I think so."

"Somewhere in there you mentioned May Gibbs. How on earth did that come about? Were you anywhere near Nutcote?"

"I spent the night there."

"That's a long way off course. "

"I think I now know more that any cicada or any human about the effects of wind on small flying creatures. I could write a thesis."

"Do you know who May Gibbs is? Is she a part of the mission?"

"She might be. I read some of her leaflet."

"I have her books somewhere." He reached up to a shelf above the desk.

"Here you go. I read this to my daughter when she comes in."

Gerry saw the drawings of the little gumnut babies on the cover.

"That's them! Snugglepot and Cuddlepie."

"Correct. Did you know that among her many characters she had a soft spot for cicadas. I don't know if she ever drew them but she writes about them. In this chapter *The Journey Begins* she says '*On a very hot night, when the cicadas were singing so loudly that Snugglepot couldn't hear his father snoring ...*'

Gerry chimed in: '... *he and Cuddlepie crept out of bed and out of the house.'*

Merac looked at him.

"I read it." said Gerry. "I want to read the whole story."

"It's here anytime you want. Somewhere else I remember she described cicadas as sounding 'like a sea of policemen's whistles.' She'd been walking in the bush."

"We can be loud when we're a crowd."

"She also had a nice character called Wise Old Kookaburra.

"That must be the one I met." said Gerry still feeling the press of the giant beak on his sides. "He saved my life. I hope I meet him again. I didn't thank him."

"Tell me about the name and the song you've brought back for us."

"Joan Sutherland is the name on the plaque. There were more names but I think that must be the one. I've heard the Botanic Gardens cicadas talk about her."

"That sounds very promising, Gerry. She was a very famous singer."

"Was?"

"She died a few years ago. She was Australian but she was famous right round the world. Probably our best ever opera singer. I wonder which role she sang that could help us."

"Can we find out?"

"I'm sure we can. But I thought she lived in the Eastern Suburbs. Hang on a sec."

Merac picked up his phone and pushed in a number from his address book.

"John? Merac ... Well thanks. You? ... Joan Sutherland, mate. Her name is on a plaque over at Cremorne. No? Never lived there? Not the same one. Oh, you've heard that one. OK. That's fine. I think the name is all the clue we need. So, tell me what were her most famous roles? When she was at her peak. Yes. I know Lucia... Yes... Yes... Oh really. Queen of the Night. The Magic Flute. Of course... That Top F... No, I won't try it myself. Thanks mate."

Merac tapped off. He walked to the piano. He opened the lid and looked at Gerry.

"Ready for this?"

He pushed a white key. A clear note rang out.

"Top F. Joan Sutherland hits it like a bell in that aria in The Magic Flute..."

Gerry's jewels glowed.

'"I can do that!" Gerry burst out. "That's the note that Max sings!"

"Who's Max?"

"The Dark Cicada."

Over the next hour, and it did take an hour, Merac sipped his chilled tap water and watched his little hero work his way steadily through a selection of saps from branches collected in the last two days. Not only was Gerry a hearty sucker, he tended to exaggerate to make a point. Apart from his detailed reporting, which Merac knew to be accurate because cicadas never lie, Gerry included descriptions of exactly how he felt at each stage as he told his story.

What a ride, thought Merac, the cicadas won't forget that.

Chapter Twenty Five

If you'd grown up in Sydney thirty or forty years ago, you'd remember the summers of your childhood. Yes, the sun did indeed shine every day. It was hot by the time you woke up grabbed some Vegemite on toast a glass of Milo and headed out. Nothing much of interest to keep you in the house. Yes, there was TV but that wasn't switched on till you came home. No computer devices to keep you from the sun and swimming, tree-climbing, bike-riding, cubbyhouse building and backyard cricket or tennis played against the side of the house or between chalk lines on quiet suburban road. Books? No, outside of school terms they were wet day things.

Things have changed, thought Dad, making some scrambled eggs. Is that a good thing? Not necessarily bad either. Just different. You wouldn't let your kids play anywhere near a road these days. Not that that would be a problem, because it's so hard to get them outside anyway. At least in school holidays you're not driving all over town taking them to sport.

It was a day like his childhood. Warm already this early in the morning. But Dad was still surprised when Tim leapt sideways into the room and jumped alongside him.

"Yeeeeesss!! What a day!"

"Morning, mate. What's so good about it?"

"What a day to be alive!"

"Never heard you say that before."

"I just heard the surf reporter on the radio say that."

"Well he's absolutely right. This is a classic Sydney summer's day. Already 25 degrees at eight o'clock. Going to be a scorcher."

"That's exactly what he said, Dad."

"I taught him all he knows."

"Sure." A gentle punch on the thigh.

Dad reached across to the radio on the window sill. He turned it on. It was tuned to a classic rock station.

"How are the girls?"

"Still in bed."

"This brekkie will get them up. They love the smell of toast in the morning."

Dad looked out the window sniffing the air, checking out the hot blue of the sky, not pure clear blue but shadowed as though through steam. "I'll tell you one thing your friend on the radio hasn't got onto yet. It's too humid to stay this way. We'll cop a storm this afternoon, I betcha."

"Oh no. We're going to the concert tonight."

"I think we'll be OK. They have a roof at the Opera House. Quite an expensive one. I think you'll find it will do the job tonight. You won't get wet and you will hear the singers."

Pulling four plates out of the cupboard, Dad heard the first chords of one of his all time greats ... good old rock and roll. He swayed his shoulders as the music bopped along, laying the plates on the bench to the beat of the guitars. Tim was sourcing cutlery and tapping it on the table. His sense of rhythm was pretty good although it was hard not to keep time with this simple beat.

Right on cue Dad started singing "Whatever you want ..."

Mum walked in and lit up at the scene. Here were her two favourite men. A sunny weekend coming up. Breakfast already on the way and that song, one of their shared favourites on the radio.

"I know that one. That's ....that's ....

Dad continued singing "...whatever you need ..."

"Yes.Yes .I'll get it."

"You know it . It's ..."

"Don't-tell-me-don't-tell-me!"

Dad was about to say the name of the group but stopped abruptly. He knew the rules of the game

had to be obeyed. The way she staccatoed those six words signalled an instant silence. He could not offer any more clues, unless she specifically requested. The memory stack in the human brain can be activated in many ways. His preferred way was to go through the alphabet. He often had a 'shape' to the words he could see in his mind and a methodical progression would sometimes give him a plausible first letter. Then another run through the alphabet for possible second letters.

Mum would take herself back to the last occasion she experienced or witnessed the name or phrase she was searching for. Sometimes the surroundings of that time or place would act as a prompt and the forgotten words would bubble up.

This morning he teased her by humming confidently as a man who not only knew the melody, he knew all the words, the name of the album, the name of each member of the group and even the time and place of the concert they had attended that she was now trying to locate in the labyrinth of her mind.

In the years they had been playing this game, actually starting before they were married, it had once taken him five days to unscramble a particular nine letter word on the daily games page of the Herald. Five days of serious thought. She later found on corners of the newspaper, even on scraps beside the bed, the nine letters in his bold and correct writing rearranged every which way but the correct way as he gnawed at it. She left the page folded open on the kitchen table. Passing by she would glance down and murmur."You know some of them really leap out at you."

Each morning she had asked sweetly; "Do you want to know? Do you want me to tell you?" or even the blunt and sarcastically triumphant: "Give in?"

"Nooo. Nooo" he wailed. A wounded man, forcing himself to soldier on, his mind returning many times during the day to the snag it was caught on.

But he finally got it. She found the word beautifully rendered on a piece of graph paper stuck under a fridge magnet.

Her record was two weeks for the name of a film.

"You know the one with that lovely English girl and Donald Sutherland in Venice."

In the two weeks she was suffering, he had forgotten about it. But she continued to grapple with it. Finally she startled him so much one morning that he scratched the paint on the car as he was about to put the key in. She shouted in triumph: "Don't Look Now!"

Status Quo continued to tantalise her as through the window Dad could see the sleek black cat padding across the paving. He flew effortlessly in three fluid jumps onto the barbecue table, onto the lower part of the wall and then up to where the top bricks disappeared under the lower leaves of the gum tree.

He stretched out his front paws, bowed and settled. Dad thought there was something on the bricks in front of him.

"What's Monty looking at?"

"He's probably talking to his cicada friend" said Tim.

"What?"

"He has a greengrocer as a friend. I've seen them talking a few times."

"Talking? What do they say to each other?"

"Well, I can't really hear anything but I guess they're talking because they sit there in the sun on top of the wall nose to nose for minutes and minutes. Then the cicada flies off."

"Are you serious?"

"Cross my heart."

"What about Ted?"

"Ted's not bothered. I'm not sure he's met the cicada, but Mont seems to enjoy catching up with his friend. He gives me a good rub or a headie if I'm there when he jumps down."

"What are you two saying about Monty?" Mum joined them at the window.

"He's up there talking to his cicada friend."

"Oh sure."

By now Ellie had joined them and picked up the last pieces of conversation.

"I believe him. Monty is an exceptional cat." As if to prove her point as they looked at the back half of their black cat, its front end filtered through the green leaves, they all heard a small sound like a cicada starting up.

"See" said Ellie. "A cicada talking to a cat."

They all laughed.

"Do you remember that cicada I told you about in the Park? The one I gave birth to?"

"Mum!"

"You know what I mean, darling. I gave him his life when I moved the rock. I wonder if that's the one Monty has made friends with. Would he still be alive? They don't live long to do they?"

"There seemed to be a lot more of them when I was a kid." Dad looked out the window. "Not just green ones, but brown and yellow, big flouries, little black ones. Even ones with a red nose."

"Rudolf!"

"We called them cherry noses. We used to bring them up out of the ground by pouring water down their holes."

"You'd drown them!"

"No, they came up and we put them on a tree and watch them come out of their shells. Their wings were all soft and scrunched up ... it was amazing to watch them dry out and unfold into these full size wings. Stiff and transparent like cellophane. Then they would crawl up higher or fly off."

"Can you show us a cicada coming out one day, Dad?"

"You probably have more chance of seeing it on YouTube than in real life. "

"I'll have a look tonight. No I won't, I'll have a look now. Ellie, coming?"

The kids ran out.

Mum turned to her husband.
"The internet has replaced life."

"Oh come on. Our kids are not too bad really."

"Yes, you're right. We do get out a lot as a family and we do work at it. They are good kids, when you see and hear about so many of them. Even some people we know are having real trouble, I mean serious, with their kids. Even at this age. What will they be like when they are teenagers? We are so lucky..."

"Good management, I reckon, more than good luck. More you than me, too."

"You're a great Dad."

"But you've done all the real work. I just lob in with a few Dad jokes every so often."

"Rubbish. Give us a hug."

"By the way did you make that phone call? To the adoption people."

"I did. The lady I spoke to was very nice, and she sent me to their website..."

"Not the internet! You'll never go outside again!"

"She took me through to a couple of pages which seem to be specific to us, to me. About someone not directly related getting the information. It seems it is difficult, not so much difficult but time consuming, a lot of letter writing and a lot of documents to provide. But it's not impossible. Among other things it asks if I have the permission of the birth mother."

"That will be difficult."

"But if I can find the proper certificates I can still get there, I think. Ultimately it's at the discretion of the department director. I can't see why a nice family like us shouldn't be successful."

"OK. What time do we have to be there tonight?"
"Is it seven or eight?"
"I'll have to check."

And so started a memorable day for the family.

Meanwhile the noise they heard was not actually a cicada talking to a cat, but a cat talking to a cicada. Gerry had flown into the higher branches of the tree as he always did as a precaution to check things out before he fluttered to the wall. He watched as Monty climbed up but he was not prepared for what happened next. Monty produced a sound remarkably like a real greengrocer. Gerry would not have believed it if he had not been watching.

"Wow. How did you do that!"

"Not easy. Something you said the other day made me wonder how far this speech and communication could go. I was practicing quietly last night. Not quite quietly enough because Ted came stalking me and also that horrible skinny white cat from over the road. At least I must have sounded authentic. So I thought I'd try in on you. Whaddyareckon?"

"Sounds great. Almost like a song."

"Well, I started with a steady purr and then sort of forced it into my throat like a sort of miauw on top of a rumble. It's difficult hitting one note and staying with it, isn't it?"

"Not for me, Monty."

"Well you're working off a fixed set of drums. I have a flexible throat to play with. I have to adjust that correctly. It's the difference between a cymbal and a violin."

"Oh, you've got tickets on yourself. Remember I have been practicing to hit a note that's quite foreign to me. It's way below my natural register. But I'm getting there."

"You must show me sometime. Now, something I meant to ask you. You were saying the other day you spend how long underground?"

"About seven years, I'm told. I don't remember all of it. Just bits. Sleeping and sapping."

"How do you know seven years is up?"

"You don't actually count. One day you wake up and just feel like letting go the roots and tunnelling upwards through the soil. You just know you'll find the light."

"How far do you have to go?"

"Not that far; about as far as your nose to your tail"

"Nasty way to get started, inside the dirt."

"You're inside a shell. That keeps the dirt out of your eyes. And when you make it up onto a tree and split your way out of the shell and feel the sun on your back as your wings open up ... it's the best day of your life. You can't wait to sing. Really let it rip. So how did you get born?"

"Don't know exactly; just woke up next to my mother one day. Couldn't see a thing, but her fur was warm and the milk was on whenever you wanted. Not bad at all really."

"Sounds nice."

"Then some strangers come and take you away and it's saucers from then on. Bit of a let down as I remember. I ate a cicada once. Well, I bit it."

"Yuk. Don't tell me that."

"I won't do it again, I assure you. Tasted horrible."

"Sap tastes good."

"So does fish. Want to go for lunch?"

Chapter Twenty Six

Beppis Restaurant in East Sydney is one of the city's institutions.

In a town where restaurants open and close every week, few have stood the test.

For scholars of fine dining it is interesting that of the respected veterans a great proportion are Italian: Darcy's, Lucio's, Machiavelli ...

But Beppis tops them all with over half a century on the same site, in the practised hands of the same family. It is not a glamorous stage to see and be seen but an intimate and friendly venue. Against a patina of dark woods and exposed brick this is a superior trattoria with white cloths, napkins folded into crisp pyramids and elegant flatware and glassware. It still serves some recipes brought from Italy in the 1950s.

One of its endearing features is the possibility of dining in one of the private rooms with walls racked from floor to ceiling with a fine selection of reds, good to great, bottles and magnums, Australian and Italian.

It is not unusual for patrons to decline the wine list and indicate a bottle or two from the wall, a remembered favourite or something never tried. For some hosts this is a gesture of genuine wine knowledge, for some a celebration - the traditional 'good day at the races' or for some just posing and showing off. Beppi's waiters have seen them all.

Over the years, these rooms had often contained Harold Scortz who at different occasions, lunch or dinner, could be categorised as any one or all three of the above.

Today was lunch.

Harold had his driver pull over into the red No Stopping zone. There was never even a thought about being booked. All but the newest parking cops knew his car and would just walk by, wishing him "G'day" if they were close enough. Even if a newcomer was inclined to give the big Mercedes a ticket or note the numberplate for an electronic fine, the matter would just dissolve in the system.

Some of them hated it, but anyone can tell you, this is a big bad town, and Harold was always at the right end of it.

He had invited Robertson Mooney, Meg and Paul to join him. His thoughts this day were more on the food and wine than the topics his guests would want discussed. Paul would know all the answers to that stuff. Leave it to him to fill in the gaps while Harold unencumbered by thought could lord it over Robertson and exercise his charms with Meg. Not that he was really serious about either activity. Robertson was a nothingburger in this town and there was no way he really fancied going any further with Meg. His flirting was not designed to achieve the usual outcome – he could not see himself spending any social time with the woman – but was just strung together to irritate her. It would be amusing as the day progressed to watch her reactions to his grubby innuendos.

He knew, and she knew, that she could not afford to be offended carrying her precious petition. Any more than Robertson could retaliate as strongly as he would like to Harold's banter. Meg knew Harold's involvement, though unofficial, was very important to the success of her proposal. She had been involved with him on many matters before. But all of those projects were council or government business where outcomes may be compromised or downright disappointing but it was all in a day's work. Nothing personal. You soldiered on. Tried another tack, looked for another way.

However what she had in her slender folder today was very personal, very close to her heart. She would do almost anything to keep it on track and to guide it through.

She hated that he could toss her ideas out like a stale bunch of flowers in a bin.

Harold made an exaggerated movement to open the rear door as his driver came around the side of the car.

"I'll get this, Jeeves. You alright there, Meg, a bit squeezy in the back? Sorry they don't make anything bigger. Hope you blokes behaved yourselves."

He took Meg's hand to assist her to the footpath. Paul had been in the middle of the back seat. He of all people was hardly likely to have been fiddling anywhere near the lady's frock.

 "Very comfortable in the back." said Robertson, straightening up.

"Oh, is it? I wouldn't know. This jalopy is getting on now, Ralston. I've had it three months. Ashtrays are nearly full so I might have to trade it."

Robertson gave a strained smile as he stepped back to look at the numberplate: *S65 AMG*

Harold caught him immediately.

"I'm not so vain as to need my initials on a numberplate like some people round here. I get the Merc blokes to stick the number of the new model on when I buy it. I just hope those German engineers don't come up with a model number the same as a NSW plate that some other bastard has already taken. Although I'm sure we could fix that."

"I'm sure you could."

"Yeah. Make the factory change the model number." Harold laughed. "Nah, just have the other bastard killed. Quicker."

The group of four stood on the heat of the footpath as the driver closed the door and walked round to get in. Harold slapped him on the back as he walked past.'

"Don't forget to give it a good wash this arvo. Never know who's been in it."

The driver hated Harold.

Could be a long day, thought Robertson.

A sudden gust of hot air had Paul looking up to the corner where he noticed a large black cat with its sleek black fur ruffling in the wind. Paul pushed his glasses up his nose. The cat seemed to have a leaf stuck on its collar as it padded towards the back of the restaurant.

Harold led them into the cool dark interior.

When they were seated, the four of them in the alcove, the waiter appeared beside Harold respectfully cradling a bottle with a maroon label.

The waiter didn't hate him. He thought he was their most obnoxious regular, but he didn't hate him.

"Is that the '98? Have you got it in a magnum?"

"Harold!"

"What's wrong? There's four of us. Couple of glasses each. They do decent glasses here. No one's in a hurry to go home, are they? It's Friday arvo for gawd's sake. Good day's work behind us. Weekend to look forward to ..."

"I wouldn't mind a white."

"OK. We'll have one of them as well. They come in magnums, champ?"

"That depends which one, sir. I think we still have a special bottling of the Katnook Chardonnay in a 3 litre."

"3 litres! Not even she could handle that! She'd be on the table doing some kind of boogie, or under it doing something worse. We'll just have a decent bottle of chardy for the young lady."

Meg wrinkled her nose ever so slightly. Harold was very quick to spot it. He had slithered up to his present position and was secured there by his ability to read people so well he knew what they felt and which way they'd jump. If they didn't jump he soon knew how to nudge them. Quickly calculating what people wanted was the skill, ignoring their wishes unless they co-incided with his was the easy part. He proudly thought of himself as part mindreader, part magician and part sewer rat.

"Not happy? Should've picked you for ABC, Meg. Anything But Chardonnay. No worries. We'll have a bottle of your Cristal, champ. Every girl likes that."

"Even if it is partly chardonnay", whispered Paul. Only the waiter heard.

They ordered and ate.

When their starters were cleared away, Meg placed her folder in front of her.
"No such thing as a free lunch" said Harold checking the level in the decanter. It was going down well, and Robertson the war hero was doing his bit, he noticed.

"Meg, you may put that away. I, we, have read you proposal. Haven't we, Paul? You may find me on some occasions a little more pro-development than your mob would like, but am I not also a sensitive human being? A man who reckons he shall never see ... how's it go... a poem more lovely than a tree. Only God can punch out one of those."

"Sweetly said, Harold." Meg stroked the stem of her champagne flute.

"We have whispered in a few ears. Not all on our side I might say. Some of them did take a little arm-twisting, but I think we can say with some confidence that your city trees will be saved for the generations to come. It may take some little time for the appropriate statutes to be in place, but you and your ladies ..." a quick glance at Robertson " ... can start on the bubbly now. As you already have. Another bottle ?"

"Well what can I say, Harold? I thought ... I thought ..."

"You thought you'd have to fight me every inch, just like that waterfront thing you got your knickers in a knot about. Not this time. It's all sweet. I don't even want anything in return. Well perhaps one small thing. Anyway. Cheers!"

They all raised their glasses.

The waiters were visibly relieved. Not all Harold's lunches ended with such accord. On some afternoons, usually much later, there had been unpleasant scenes with things broken. Even scuffling and on one occasion fists were thrown. Recompense was never a problem but it was a trifle tedious tidying up before the evening setting.

As Meg put down her empty glass, it shattered.

It was so unexpected and the shock to all of them was so great that they were not aware that there had been a loud and piercing note from the direction of the kitchen a split second before the glass exploded.

Gerry encouraged by Monty had managed to settle perfectly on High F.

The cat Paul had noticed in the laneway before they entered was indeed Monty. The leaf on his neck was Gerry, hitching a ride as the two headed off for lunch.

Although he was perfectly fed at home, Monty couldn't resist the occasional adventure with a promise of interesting food at the end of it. Ted no longer moved from the courtyard. He had all he needed in that small paved square, summer or winter, but Monty's spirit of youth easily lifted him over the wall, over a few more backyards, a few more walls, across a laneway and another wall to the back door of Beppi's restaurant. The kitchen staff knew him now after their first meeting a couple of summers ago when he miaowed up to them while they were having a breath of air in the laneway.

For Monty there was always a good neck rub and a few pieces of leftover fish to be had.

His arrival today with Gerry on board did create a stir. One of the dishwashers tried to take Gerry from his neck but a quick swipe of the paw and an uncharacteristic growl soon let him know that was not on.

"Oh, so he's your friend. OK, we won't touch him. Would you like a piece of fish?"

"Do you mind if I tuck in?" Monty asked Gerry.

"No problem. I'll get some sap back at your tree later."

The dishwasher heard nothing of course but could have sworn the cat shook his head when he asked: "What would your friend like? Some salad?"

Monty wasn't about to show he could understand let alone talk to these chaps. He must stay in dumb animal character if these free food visits were to be maintained. Imagine if they thought they had a talking cat on their hands. He'd be on the evening news before you could say "flathead fillet."

The warmth coming from the kitchen had Gerry fired up for a little song. He hadn't had a good sing all day. He fluttered off the black fur and sat beside the bowl of fish as Monty ate.

The cat looked up with his huge golden eyes and noted Gerry's agitation.

"Have you been practicing that note you told me about?"

"I have."

"Can you hit it? It's very high for a soprano isn't it?"

"It's quite low for us cicadas."

"You want to give it a go now?"

"Here?"

"Sure, it will give the boys here a kick. Just step over there away from my eardrums and go for it, champ."

Gerry skidded across the glossy floor into the doorway. He produced a couple of scratchy warm up notes then went for it. He was too high to start but settled back to the right frequency and gave it all he had.

At 120 decibels it sliced the aromatic air of the kitchen. What a note! A true pinnacle for a good opera singer.

Harold, Paul and Robertson were open mouthed. Robertson was the first to reach forward but with the back of her hand covered in small pieces of glass, Meg's reaction was surprising to them all.

"That was a Top F." she laughed. "I never believed those stories, and now I've seen it with my very own eyes."

"You're going to need new glasses." Paul said dryly.

"Who *do* you have in that kitchen? Joan Sutherland?" Robertson asked the waiter who was already approaching with a small pan and brush. The other waiter had a new champagne flute ready to place.

"I'll go and see sir."

By the time he arrived in the preparation area, all he could see was the kitchen hands laughing as they looked towards the outside door.

He missed the flash of black fur as Monty with Gerry clinging on leaped the closest wall in the laneway opposite.

"Wow, Gerry, that was amazing."

"I hope you are allowed back in there."

"I'll be fine. I'll go back in a couple of days. I just thought we shouldn't stick around in case we were identified with broken glass and screaming. The boss may not find it as funny as we do, but it will blow over, mostly because no one will believe it."

"I suppose that not what they expect in their restaurant."

"Did you know you could break a wine glass like that?"

"No idea."

"Now we know. You're a champ, Gerry."

The waiter reported back to the table. Meg thought it was all a hoot now she had a new glass in her hand.

"I'm told it was a cat and a cicada, sir."

"Really. Is that what they said they saw? What are they drinking back there? I thought we were the ones getting sloshed."

"Whoever it was, they have gone now madam. I'm sure it won't happen again."

Meg turned to Robertson.

"Just remind me to put my glass down well before we go in on Saturday night."

"Saturday night?" asked Harold innocently.

"We are going to the Opera."

"The Magic Flute," said Robertson "There's a special performance from New York."

"Is that the one that's been adapted for the young audience?" asked Paul.

"That's the one. They've shortened it a little I believe, left out some of the more obscure references and dialogue, and provided some amazing sets and costumes the littlies should enjoy. The lady behind the Lion King designed it. "

"Saturday night?" said Harold looking at Paul, who knew what the glance meant and nodded imperceptibly.

"If it's for kids, why are you there?"

"We're taking my nieces."

"Ah yes" said Harold as a familiar feeling suffused his body. Not the red wine, it was time for a sneaky move, thoroughly prepared, and now waiting to be played.

"You're on the board of directors, aren't you?"

"I am"

"That would entitle you to some special privileges would it not?"

"Some."

"Parking?"

"I am given a spot at the top of the carpark when I'm attending a show."

"You look like you're in a pretty good mood right now?"

"Oh Harold, I'm floating."

"Would you do something for me?"

"Almost anything. If you ask me today."

Paul watched the game unfold. This was only a small favour his boss was chasing but he'd seen the same tactics used to stop or start an expressway construction, add a couple more floors to a city high rise or chew the corner off a national park for apartment blocks and a golf course.

"Would it be OK if I took your spot on Saturday night? I will make arrangements for you. Anything you like. I can pick you up in my car or buy you a stretch limo there and back. The young'uns would like that. Hotel rooms in the city if you want. Dinner at Guillaume? Aria? Quay? Est ? ..."

With her eyes fixed on his, Meg held out her glass for more Roederer. They all watched the foam swirl and settle. You could hear a bubble rise.

"Are *you* going to the opera that night?"

"Wouldn't miss it for quids."

"Then why wouldn't you take a limo, have a lovely meal and stay in the city?"

"Long story. I'd like to show the car to a friend of mine who will be in town. Visiting from overseas. I'll need to make a quick getaway so a park at the top is worth gold to me."

Meg looked across at Robertson who could only shrug.

"He's not the boss. Are you Ricardo? Your car space. Meg. Your decision."

Robertson ignored him, "The girls in a limo could be fun..."

"Very well, Harold. I can't see why not. We'll do it. I can arrange that and let you have the details."

"Good. More wine anyone. Paul, you keeping your eye on that decanter?"

Over dessert Harold asked Robertson about his military service and listened between mouthfuls to some polite but underwhelming stories. Harold already knew more about the man than he could have volunteered in an hour.

The lunch quietened and faded. Paul went out the front and made sure the car was there and sorted out the bill. The food was great. The wine was great. The tip was huge.

Everyone had what they wanted.

As it happened Meg and Robertson took a taxi back over the Bridge to the North Shore. Harold and Paul settled in the back of the Mercedes.

"That was well played."

"Thankyou Paul. A little bit lucky the way it came up but you grab them when you can, eh matey?"

Harold chuckled. Paul smiled. It didn't need saying between them, but Paul finally voiced it.

"Why would anyone park their half million dollar car right where a bomb's going off if they knew there was a bomb going off there."

Chapter Twenty Seven

"I've had enough of this shite. I'm going for a walk. I may be some hours."

"You're not going to that dreadful Mercantile place are you."

"And why not? I'm sick of being up to my eyeballs with these posh pricks. They're worse than New York. They won't leave me alone."

"Sean, you are a guest in this country."

"And sure I'm grateful and happy to be here. I signed up for the performances and the rehearsals, the meeting and the greeting, but not every minute of me feckin' life. I'll go mad if I can't be among some normal people for an hour or two."

The Visiting Conductor, now in his fourth week in Sydney, had had a very successful morning. Rehearsals were proceeding well and he was more than happy with his orchestra and soloists.

But as he walked down the corridors of the Opera House for a quiet moment, looking for an exit to the outside air, he was set upon by photographers and journalists from the women's magazines.

Sydney society had discovered him. He transcended their idea of an orchestra leader. He was not a pompous old man with unkempt white hair around a florid face; he was attractively young and darkly handsome. Although they knew he had his very presentable wife with him they were chasing him as often as they could, scouring for the scandal. The gossips were referring to him as Conductor McDreamy.

He left the building.

He walked out under the spreading steps of the main concourse and took the opening to the left towards the staircase that would take him to the top of the Tarpeian Cliff. He wanted to have a look at those two trees he'd passed every day from his hotel in Macquarie Street on his way to the House. Someone had told him they were special.

As he climbed he noticed some workmen placing those orange witches hats around the path at the top of the cliff. He thought it odd that it took two of them to take each one off the handcart and place it carefully near the edge. Different cities, different practices.

The day after Gerry's epic flight Merac asked him to meet at the Red Twins. Checking his calendar the day before, he found himself vaguely wondering when he could get his work moving again. He could only think of Gerry. Then he realised that his work *was* Gerry and, for as long as his little friend survived, Gerry was his work.

Merac sat on the grass just outside the tanbark under the trees as Gerry paraded up and down his shirt across his shoulders behind his neck and back again.

"Would you like to get something to drink?" asked Merac.

"I just had a huge sap before you got here. I arrived early to give myself time. I seem to be getting thirstier as I get older. Could that be right?"

"We all get older, Gerry. You know that none of us live forever."

"You humans look older as you get older don't you? We don't, do we? We stay the same. Was I ever a child? I don't remember being one."

"Seven years ago you were very small. You started as an egg just like us. I suppose you could say you used to be a child. But after those early years underground you come to the surface, pop out of your shell, and then you don't change much for the rest of your life. But then you don't have a lot of time to get old like we do. And you don't have a lot of time to do things. Especially doing something as good as you have done, starting with your Quest. That's why these last few days are so important."

"What few days? *My* last few days?"

"No, not *your* last few days. I mean these last few days when you've been on your Quest. We're hoping it will be important for generations to come."

"I'm interested in children. Monty has some children in his house. I've seen them but I haven't met them. Tell me about your child. When does she know as much as you do?"

"Human children learn very slowly. They grow very slowly. A child is a work in progress. They take years to acquire wisdom but *you* seem to have arrived knowing everything."

"No I don't. I learn some new things every day. I really do."

"Oh I know you do. But somehow you already understand the basics, you've fitted straight into the shape of our lives. That must have been passed down from somewhere. My belief is that wisdom is hereditary. Maybe not so much in the individual but in the total knowledge of overlapping generations. Whatever has happened to any one of us before is now in us all."

Gerry walked quickly to Merac's shoulder ready to take off, trembling with excitement.

Merac continued.

"I believe that parents live on in their children. And in turn in *their* children. I'm not a religious man, but I find myself agreeing with some of the sentiments expressed at funerals. We never really die as long as someone remembers us. We humans have the advantage of writing things down, or drawing them, or videoing them these days. All *your* knowledge seems to be inherent and intuitive."

"That's just what I said to Max!" Gerry was fluttering in front of Merac's face. "Do you believe that too?"

Merac held out his hand and Gerry landed, still watching the face in front of him.

"I do, Gerry."

"What's it like to grow old?"

"You're asking me? I don't think of myself as growing old."

"But you've seen people who have."

"It seems to be a process of awareness over many years. Some aspects of it seem to be welcome at first but then it gets nastier towards the end. People begin to add up how many things they've done for the last time or will never do. I've seen serene characters like my mother accepting gracefully, and others like my father raging all the way. You're lucky ... I don't think you'll ever experience it."

"I won't grow old?"

"You won't live forever, Gerry. You won't be just as you are now. But you will be in people's memories. You are special, you and your friends. You're all good. I think in a way you are better than us. I've seen no evil in any of you. You may not live forever on the planet, but you will in my mind. You're not just little creatures to me. I reckon you're much more. I've seen you as Spitfires and Pavarottis; Einsteins and Mandrakes; Lancias and Ghandis."

"I don't know any of those cicadas."

"There not cicadas. They're other things that I think are good looking or fast or thrilling or clever. They're not making many more like them. Just like you."

Gerry flew back up to Merac's shoulder as a tall dark and handsome stranger walked up to the sign at the base of the Twin Reds. He looked directly at Merac with a polite smile. Then down at the sign. He took a minute to read:

Sydney's oldest trees?

Forest Red Gums (Eucalyptus tereticornis) like these could have grown here on the rocky sandstone foreshores of Sydney Harbour when the Royal Botanic Gardens and Domain were established in 1816.

We do not know whether these two trees were alive at the time or whether they are direct descendants that grew up sometime later in the 19th Century when parts of this site still had wild bushland. Regardless, these are probably the closest oldest, native trees to the centre of Sydney.

The Trust treasures its remnants as much as its 3000 planted specimens.

His eyes moved to the map on the right of the sign.

Sydney's real bushland treasures are on the harbour headlands and foreshores, some of which you can see from here. This map shows nearby places where you can experience bushland and landscapes as they existed prior to 1816.

"They are a fine old age, are they not?"

"Some botanists think the Trust is being modest and they could have been here before the English settlement. Possibly over 300 years old."

"Is that right?"

"I read it somewhere."

"You're interested in the native bushland then?"

"Yes, I am." He's a pleasant enough bloke thought Merac. Irish I'd say.

"I can see you've an affinity with the wildlife."

Merac raised an eyebrow.

"That little creature on your shoulder there. He's certainly the right colour for my liking."

Merac reached up as Gerry moved further under his collar.

"That'll be one of your cicadas."

"It is indeed. Gerry, come on out and meet someone. I'm sure he won't hurt you."

"Not even a fly."

Gerry squawked involuntarily as Merac had to prise his little feet from the fabric.

"Gerry is a male Greengrocer. The males are the ones that make the noise, I mean the song. They do it simply to attract the females. Is that right, Gerry?"

Gerry of course didn't answer. He was not sure if the stranger would be able to understand him but he paraded importantly around Merac's hand. He even thought of clearing his tymbals and giving a quick burst to demonstrate that singing could exist outside of courtship.

"Aaah, love is all around us. I hear them in full song when I walk through the Gardens in the mornings."

"Are you visiting Sydney?"

"I am that. Just for a few weeks. I'm a guest in your House down there."

The stranger gestured elegantly with his long supple hands.

"The Opera House?"

"To be sure."

Merac had read the papers. The penny dropped and he was confident enough to ask.

"Are you by any chance conducting?"

"I am."

"I think we will be seeing you tomorrow night down there. The Magic Flute?"

"The very same."

Reassured he was in the right company, Gerry thought he'd let one rip. Starting with a touch of crackle he soon smoothed out to a carefully modified note, lower than his usual register. It was the note he had been practising, the pure song of the Dark Cicada.

The Visiting Conductor fell back a step, well taken in mirth.

"By God. The little fellow knows his notes. That'll be a Top F. I usually hear it from one of my sopranos. In the Magic Flute, as it happens."

"Perhaps he knew that." said Merac straight faced. "When he heard us mention it."

"What a little charmer. Could I hold him?"

"Sure. His name's Gerry."

"You're fecking with me. He really has a name?"

The Conductor held out his hand palm up to Merac's and Gerry climbed obligingly across. He remained calm as he was lifted up to eye level and he liked the look of that smile. If Merac likes him, I like him.

"A very pretty green if I may say, it reminds me of..."
"You're not going to say a Kerry hillside, are you?"

The Conductor laughed as Gerry jiggled in his hand. "No I was going to say my wife's eyes."

"Red hair?"

"No, black. Still a classic Irish colouring. Since the Armada anyway."

Both men thought of their wives.

The moment of tranquillity was broken by the sound of a cicada starting up in the tree not that far above.

It surprised the three of them.

"Now that'll be a lot higher up the register. There's not been a soprano alive could hit that note."

Gerry and Merac recognised the regular call of a young greengrocer.

They both spotted him at the same time. Gerry took off to investigate. 'Who's that singing in *my* tree?'

Moving slightly to the side, Merac pointed out three small green shapes as Gerry joined another two on a branch just below the lowest bunch of leaves.

Gerry approached the singer who paused his song and said: "I saw Merac down there, and I thought I'd say hello"

"You know Merac?" said Gerry.

"We met him at his hospital and he brought us back here because our tree had been paved. We've been down in the Domain but they're a very tight crowd down there. Not too friendly with strangers.

They think they're special just because they can see the Opera House. Some of the young ones were quite rude to us. We're not great joiners so we looked around and saw these trees up here. We flew in earlier this morning and we saw you arrive and have a drink. I kept quiet and we stayed out of the way until we were sure who you were. We had no idea that Merac would turn up. You must be Gerry? Merac told us you were going to do a Quest. Oh, by the way, I'm Giles and this is my sister Gwendolene."

"Pleased to meet you. This is actually the tree where I emerged."

"That's wonderful. You don't mind us being here?" Gwendolene spoke up clearly. Unusual for a girl to be so bold at first meeting. Gerry liked that, and looked at her with interest. She was very pretty, a very purebred green.

"Not at all. Help yourself. It's good sap. Quite mature. I'll show you around if you like."

"So when is the Quest?" asked Giles.
"I've done it."

"Really."

"I was able to give Merac and Cir Franklin what they wanted, I think. So now I'm just another cicada with time on his hands. All summer just to hang around."

"I'd like to catch up with Merac. Why don't I do that now and you two can have a chat. I'm sure Gwen would like to hear all about your adventure."

"Fine by me" said Gerry looking closely at Gwendolene. Were those jewels of hers glowing? Is she a bit my way? She took a couple of steps closer.

Giles fluttered down to the two men below landing on Merac's shoulder.

"He's back" said the Conductor. "You train them well."

Merac took the little creature onto his hand.

"Actually this is a different one. His name is ...."

Merac bent his head so he could hear the cicada whisper.

"...Giles. Of course. This is Giles."

"Now you are pulling my leg. And you accuse us of the blarney."

"No I'm not. Giles was the one singing up there. His natural range is in a higher register. Probably around four or five kilohertz."

"Will he do it again? I'd love to have a close look at how he does it?"

"I'm sure Giles won't mind. Not too loud, mate. Just so that Sean can watch you in action."

Merac held his index finger vertically and Giles climbed it. He settled with his feet pinching gently on the skin and began to sing. He'd already warmed up so hit the note exactly, although as softly as he could, and still produce a clear sound without breaking into a squawk.

The Conductor moved in closer, gobsmacked at the power of this tiny musical marvel, his mind racing to compare it with any instruments he had ever come across, orchestral or primitive. He could think of nothing that made so much pure sound with so little apparent effort. He could discern no expression on the face of course but he could see the whole body, tight as a violin string, alert and at attention as Giles poured it out. He could just observe the vibrations in the pale curved saucers of the tymbals under the green thorax.

"Amazing. You could build a symphony around a tuned set of these. Perhaps not a symphony, but certainly a triumphal piece, a grand entry. A cicada quartet would have a lot to say for itself. It would certainly attract attention."

"You'd have to put dinner jackets on them."

"To be sure that could be arranged. My tailor in Dublin is a most meticulous man."

Above them they heard the same note, sung much louder. Gerry was showing off to Gwendolene. Giles stopped his song and backed down the finger to the palm.

He and Merac both had an idea what might be happening up there.

"So it's only the male who sings." mused the Conductor looking up. He appeared to be not far behind. "The female homes in on the song. And ....?"

"Love finds a way."

The Conductor looked up the tree. They could make out only one green shape. He nodded slowly smiling.

"I think Love is finding a way."

Chapter Twenty Eight

The Sydney Opera House has a curious and turbulent history.

But probably no more so than many amazing buildings round the world, past and present.

In 2003 its designer Jorn Utzon received architecture's highest accolade, the Pritzker Prize. The citation stated: "There is no doubt that the Sydney Opera House is his masterpiece. It is one of the great iconic buildings of the 20th century, an image of great beauty that has become known throughout the world - a symbol for not only a city, but a whole country and continent."

It is nice. The city cicadas love it.

What is most amazing is that it was ever completed. Like any important project in life, it involved a journey. Highs and lows. Disappointment and determination. Good guys and bad guys.

In the 1950s a suitable building was needed to replace the ageing tram sheds on Bennelong Point. The members of the government of the day were not noted for their love and generous support of the arts, but some wise heads recognised that this site, on the side of the horseshoe-shaped bay now known as Circular Quay, facing the already iconic Harbour Bridge could actually be quite important.

The Quay covers the spot where the first white settlers set foot to establish a colony on January 26th 1788. This is the very birthplace of the country now known as Australia.

An Opera House? Seriously? Mercifully this was way before Harold's time or the world could now be contemplating some very expensive apartments.

But an Opera House it was to be.

An international competition called for entries in 1955. The short list showed some fine structures, some squarely modern, some a little more embellished in the classical tradition of European Opera Houses, some taking their cue from the maritime location and evoking great passenger liners. Over 200 entries were received. The story goes that as the jury were deliberating on the "classicals" one of the panel pulled Utzon's drawings out of the reject pile.

His "outrageous" masterpiece was chosen in 1957 and construction started in 1959.

Even as the foundations and the ochre-coloured base were well under construction, there was still no way known to man that the magic outline, the striking essential of the structure, the rearing white sails could actually be built.

The contractors were desperately experimenting with lightweight concrete, poured on site. The Romans had cracked it with the Pantheon a few thousand years earlier so it couldn't be that hard.

But it was.

That is, until the early 60s when Utzon steepened the profile of his original sketches and made every curve a segment of a sphere. He demonstrated his new sails by cutting up an orange. Work now raced ahead and Sydneysiders ooed and aahed as 'their' building rose.

Politics in Sydney is never far from anything. This now world city was founded as a penal settlement to help empty England's jails, where you could be imprisoned for many years for stealing even a morsel of bread. The bones of this town, the foundations of its society, were with few exceptions formed by petty criminals, their jailers and the rougher ends of the military.

The politics got Utzon. Midway through construction there was a change of government. Outrage erupted at the soaring costs of the soaring sails. They said he was a dreamer. They needed to be practical. Impossible demands and conditions led to his resignation. His building was finished by others, very skilled and competent others, but it will never quite be his building. His vision certainly. But not entirely as he dreamed it.

The SOH was opened by Queen Elizabeth II on October 30th 1973.

Sketchy original estimates of less than $20 million had gone right over $100 million, but, shoosh, Her Majesty's here, mustn't grumble.

Beethoven's Symphony Number Nine was performed.

The first opera performed in the now inadequate Opera Theatre, which as a result of more chest puffing, snarling and dog fighting by the political boys had been swapped with the much larger Concert Hall halfway through construction, was Prokofiev's War and Peace.

Harold Scortt waved his pass at the attendants at the entrance to the underground carpark.

They would possibly have allowed that car through anyway. Certainly one look at Harold's ruddy smile above his black bow tie would have convinced them. He rolled silently to a space right near the top of the ramps which double-helixed into the depths of the Sydney sandstone. This desirable parking spot assured you of an easy getaway after the show. If indeed that is what you had planned.

Meg and her girls were already in one of the bars. French champagne for her, not house. Diet cola for them. She looked around and saw some patrons she knew. A smile and an incline of the head was all that was required. If special friends made it through the crush, her position at the bar would ensure a glass of bubbles could quickly be served.

Dad, Mum, Ellie and Tim had walked from home a couple of kilometres away; they were all fit and healthy and it was a lovely summer evening. The sudden storm in the afternoon had cooled things down considerably from the heat of the day. There were puddles of water to be avoided as they walked.

"You fed the cats?"

"I did" said Tim.

"Did you use the sharp knife?"

"Yep"

"Ellie did you watch him?"

"Daaad. He's done it before. He's very careful, you should know that, probably better than me."

"But not as pretty."

Dad put an arm round both of his kids. Gently on Ellie's shoulders, his hand sliding under her shiny brushed hair. More roughly around Tim's neck giving him a shake as he gripped the upper arm.

They joined the crowds funnelling up the stairs. They were not nearly as young as Dad and Mum thought they would be. Of course there were many kids but much more than half of the audience would have been older. Parents and grandparents fussing and herding were obvious, however there were several couples over there in full evening dress. Old habits. The regulars, the subscription holders, weren't going to miss this. And they were going to see it their way. They may harrumph and complain at the shortening of the libretto and the more colourful Hollywood inspiration of the costumes and sets, they may even write a letter to the Herald, but they had read the reviews that assured them that the magic of Mozart was still on show; the orchestra was fine and the performers exceptional.

As long as the children didn't fiddle with their lolly wrappers. Or these days, heaven help us, text on their phones.

Dr and Mrs Matrices attracted attention as they patiently worked their way through the throng. They were a tall and handsome couple who would have been noticed in their own right, but Merac had a sleeping child in his arms partly draped over his shoulder. Not a baby either, a seven year old girl, very pretty indeed in repose. Sondrine had dressed her in a new party outfit with new little strappy shoes too. They made it up to the box office where Merac had organised to collect the tickets.

"Is your little girl OK?"

"Yes thanks, just sleeping. She'll wake up when it's important."

They would have been happy to take it in turns cradling her in their laps, she wasn't very big for her age, but the House had rules and they bought her her own seat. Merac was so happy to just be here, to be holding his daughter, to be taking her to something he knew she would enjoy.

The audience took their places and the lights went down with the opening bars from the orchestra. Not the full overture, but seasoned opera goers moved their heads slightly, singing internally along with the maestros in front of them. First timers stared with eyes wide and mouths open, some chewing tiny fists as they moved in their seats trying to take in the absolute intensity of it all as the curtain was raised.

At the end of the row Sondrine made sure her daughter was settled comfortably asleep between them.

Tamino, Pamina, Papageno and the Queen of the Night made their appearances. Birds and children flew. Towering bears danced. Choruses sang.

The Queen's famous second aria was thrilling. Smug smiles of approval from the seasoned watchers. Surprise and delight for the newcomers. Lala lala la la la! This was opera!

Pix stirred. Sondrine thought she heard her seat squeak a little. Her touch on Merac's arm was not needed. He had heard something too and looked across at the child. In the semi-darkness, brushed with received lighting from the stage, could he see the faintest smile on the child's lips?

Was the magic working?

The opera over, the crowd had applauded thunderously. The Visiting Conductor was mightily pleased especially with his soprano. As he took his several bows he scanned the audience and saw his cicada friend with his wife and their little girl who seemed to have fallen asleep.

That's a shame. I hope she heard some of it.

With tingling palms the mob poured out.

Eyes and ears tingling too, still fresh with extraordinary visions and sounds. A perfect storm of pyrotechnics, a fountain of light and sound lingered in overfilled retinas and eardrums. Delivered in masterly fashion by composer and designer holding hands across a double century gap, The Magic Flute had impressed them like a lightning strike. It would not fade quickly.

Laughter everywhere. Smiles, excited chatting. Children with upturned faces weaving, dancing , bumping into each other and squealing to be heard by the adults. Their brains were so full of colour and movement they had to let it out by replaying it. Out in the forecourt the streams spread out. Some of the more formally dressed patrons headed to the waterside bars;

no hurry for them, plenty of time for a drink or three and a mature perhaps cynical evaluation of the show tonight. Others, those with the still quivering kids, had suburbs to go to. Late dinners to prepare, some struggle with bedtime and for some an early start for work tomorrow. They were hurrying to transport, buses or trains or ferries. You'd be lucky to find a cab.

Mum and Dad watched their two running towards the harbour wall at the edge of the Quay. They wanted to check out the ferries, to see if the Lady Northcott was there.

She took his hand.

"Would you like a drink?" he said. "We can go to the bar down there."

"No it's packed, it'd be a nightmare. You know I won't queue for anything. You'd wait an hour then it'd be fifty bucks a glass."

"Well not quite. OK, we'll have a glass of wine when we get home. It's not a school day tomorrow."

"I've been thinking about my sister's baby."

"Yes?"

"I'm not going to go any further with it. I've thought about it a lot. Since I found out I've talked to a few friends and I've looked up a lot of stories on the internet. The most depressing statistic is that something like only 1 in 10 of the adopted kids actually want to see you. And even less than that manage a relationship that lasts much longer than the first meeting. And that's with their birth mothers. I've been trying to put myself into that first meeting. I stick out my hand and say: 'Hullo, You don't know me but I'm the sister of that woman who gave you away years ago. How do you do.' Do you think a seven year old would respond positively to that?"

"That's a bit harsh, but I know what you mean. Could you find out the details now and maybe leave it a few years before you make the call?"

"I thought of that. An older child would be more mature, but they'd also be more settled in their life. You never know if they've been told they are adopted. You just assume they're with a good family... they'd have to be with all the screening they go through. But what is my arrival going to do to them? A birth mother you can understand, but a sister is just a stickybeak."

"Again you're being harsh..."

"But you just don't know. And why am I doing it anyway. For her? For me? What can I add to her life? I scarcely knew my sister later in the piece, when she had the baby. Obviously never met the father. Don't even know who he is. That would be one of the first questions she'd ask, wouldn't it? All I can tell her is something about our early childhood, which wasn't too flash anyway. And what about the effect on our kids?"

"They'd love a new cousin. They don't have a lot of them."

"We may not even get close. She or her adoptive parents could have put a veto on being contacted, which they can do depending when she was adopted. She could even be dead."

"Didn't think of that."

"If she was mine, Heaven help us, I'd go through every possible alley way, and I'd be ready for the rejection. But I'm not sure I'm achieving anything here outside of satisfying my curiosity. Of course it would be great if we ended up real friends. But the chance of that is a million to one."

"Would you like me to have a go? The initial stuff anyway."

"You wouldn't get very far. I have to sign everything."

"So that's it?"

"Yes, my darling. That is it."

Mum gave Dad a hug as they looked at their kids hanging over the rail, laughing together.

"All I hope is that she has found a really nice family. And she has a long and happy life ahead of her, like our two."

Merac was carrying is beloved daughter across the forecourt, towards the entrance to the carpark when he paused halfway across and pointed Sondrine to the top of the cliff.

"See those two trees?" he said.

"I saw them as we were coming in. Lovely aren't they. I felt really drawn to them. They look sort of noble up there. Much taller and straighter, not as convoluted as most of the red gums you see around."

"They're Forest Red Gums. And we're very lucky to have them. They could be the only trees round here that were growing before the white man came. Botanists at the Gardens have done tests and they think they could be 300 years old. The local Aboriginals would have seen them grow. The trees would have witnessed the First Fleet come in. Heaven knows why they weren't cut down for firewood or building in the early days. I'm surprised they're still with us."

She took his arm and stroked their girl's neck. "I'm glad they are. I'm not feeling very modern right now. I'm in a kind of centuries-old mood, you know, that music, very happy with what the past still can still give us..."

They had just moved off again towards the carpark when it happened.

A noise neither of them would ever forget.

A clear pure note from high on the cliff. A solo cicada. No warm up, no scratching to clear the tymbals. Straight on to it. A pure Top F. Assured and confident with all the power of a singer at the peak of their career.

Merac and Sondrine turned towards the source.

So did Pix.

She stretched and squirmed in her father's arms.

"She's awake."

As they held her between them, with Sondrine hovering wordlessly over her daughter's fluttering eyes, with catching throats they drew in the beauty of her shy smile. And they did not hear another sound.

Certainly not the tinkle of a beer bottle hitting concrete from somewhere near the entrance to the Opera House carpark.

Chapter Twenty Nine

In the last few days as he was perfecting it, Gerry's song had broken a few pieces of glass but none so important as the empty longneck bottle of Reschs Pilsener that Guy and Barry had wired as their main transmitter. It was designed to connect by radio waves to the primed detonators they pushed into the Semtex they had laboriously packed into witches hats around the edge of the cliff and the entrance to the carpark.

Later that night after the crowds had gone, Barry and Guy, who would have clocked off and closed down as usual, would be in a pub well down the road when Guy would hit the button on his disposable mobile.

From there they would take two cars, one was to drive north and one south to their new lives on the beach, looking forward to endless fishing and beer drinking. They each had a favourite town where they were known at the local RSL and Surf Club. They would fit in easily as long as they didn't pull out too much money in one go. Newly arrived retirees who could afford a small shout were not uncommon in these little communities and would soon be part of the furniture, but a big-noting, big-spending city slicker would probably cause the local lads to have a quiet word with the local law.

Perhaps some time in the future when all this had died down Barry and Guy would visit each other. Tonight they just had to finish the job. It was not a matter of honour. Even though the man who hired them was a neat little Pom, they knew that above him would be some very nasty, very vindictive person. They had not and would never meet him but he would certainly have them hunted down if they failed to deliver. That didn't bear thinking about. In their minds the much lesser evil was blowing up half of Sydney, rather than the thud of a sawnoff shotgun butt on a bedroom door in the middle of the night.

They had their money. Well, half of it, which could still fund a very comfortable retirement for as long as these two expected to live. All they had to do was push the button and push off.

Unfortunately Gerry's superb song had broken the beer bottle they had used as a transmitter container just for a laugh. As they wired it up Barry had commented that the bottle seemed lighter than usual. Had the mighty brewing company been experimenting with lightweight bottles to save the planet? Or was this just a faulty one that had slipped through the system? Maybe it was perfectly normal. Barry had never held an empty one for long before.

Anyway Gerry's song got to it. It shattered as it fell from its ledge leaving the vital components strewn on the driveway surrounded by little pieces of brown glass. Not an easy fix, even if it had been noticed and attended to it at the time. Much more difficult when hours later you are in a pub down the road on your sixth schooner, with each one growing more and more confident in your abilities.

When after midnight Guy finally yanked the phone from his trouser pocket after three sticky-fingered attempts, he dropped it on the floor of the bar. Just as well Barry was in the dunny at the time. The phone seemed alright when Guy picked it up, lighting up normally when he pushed the ON button. He had the number of the transmitter on speed dial. When Barry returned he was ready. He held the phone up as though he was making a call.

"Give it a go, old son."

"A toast first."

They raised their glasses.

"To a long and happy retirement."

"Long and happy retirement."

Guy pushed the call button.

They were well over a kilometre away from the bomb. But you should have heard it fifty kilometres away.

They heard nothing.

Guy pushed the call button again. And again.

He checked the number on the screen. He also had written it on his wrist. He checked it against that. He pushed again.

Barry grabbed the phone and redialled from the number on Guy's wrist. He pressed Call.

Still nothing.

The both turned to the bar and took up their beers starting straight ahead.

"Are you going back up there?"
"Nah, I'm not going back."

They finished that beer in silence.

Barry stuck out his paw and Guy took it with his left.

"Looks like every man for himself. I might just get a start. Don't reckon I'll go straight there tonight A pity, they reckon it would have been a good weekend on the beach. Maybe I'm gunna head out west for a start. Might try a few motels for a few days."

"Smart thinking. I'll do likewise."

As it turned out, although they lived in fear for many years, they were never pursued because

their unknown patron, who would assuredly have become their lethal nemesis, found himself in circumstances which prevented him taking further action.

When Barry failed to turn up at the carpark the next morning the police were called in to examine a curious collection of items including a number of loaded witches hats. That end of the city was closed down for many hours as the bomb squad sorted things out.

When finally allowed back into his Macquarie Street offices, Harold was greeted by Paul with the sort of look on his face Harold had noted only a few times before. Paul didn't smile very often but this was more than glum.

"Before you tell me, you'd better fetch a bottle. Maybe two."

"I have already decanted one of our last magnums from '82."

"That bad, huh?"

It was early afternoon and Harold would already have been monumentally grumpy having missed a lunch. When he was informed he could not go into his building because of the bomb scare, he was now purple in face and mood. The 'No Bloody Bomb' Scare was more like it. If he could wield an axe, heads would be rolling down Macquarie Street like footballs.

"As soon as I walked in I took a call from the bank." Paul said.

"Which bank?"

"The one that really matters to us."

"Oh yeah?"

"It was the CEO himself."

Paul had set one end of the table with just one place, not wishing to presume on what he knew would be a very interesting afternoon. He had also failed to hear the bomb go off.

"Get yourself a glass." said Harold waving at the next chair.

Paul cleared his throat ready for the assault on his ears and his palate. A large glass of substantial red was not his preferred way to start this day. On any other occasion he would have quite enjoyed evaluating and savouring their last bottle of the first vintage of John Riddoch. He took a substantial gulp and continued.

"The bank it appears is looking into some irregularities ...."

""Of course there are some thumping great irregularities but I, we, pay good money to have them regularised. What went wrong, apart from the bloody bomb!"

"I don't know about the bomb yet. I will investigate. But I believe this bank thing could be even more explosive."

"That would not be hard."

"He wanted to speak to you of course, but as he had met me with you before, he gave me just a little background. He said he had some people in his office: Reserve Bank, Foreign Investment Review Board, Commonwealth Police and ASIC."

"Right. In itself that's serious, but not terminal, Paul."

Reaching for the decanter Harold sounded remarkably calm. Paul knew the import of what he was about to say and, unflappable Englishman that he was, saw absolutely no justification for calm.

"He mentioned some of our, um, other accounts. In particular DefianceTrust, Take That Nominees and UpYours2..."

"Shit. How did they get onto that?" Paul took another large mouthful.

He's right, Harold thought, much worse that a fizzled bomb.

"I have your passport on your desk and I have spoken to the airline. There is a small suitcase near the door" Paul hoped he had judged it right.

"I saw it on the way in, thanks Paul. I was going to say, you keep the Merc, which is obviously still sitting un-bloody-scathed in the carpark. But I think under the circumstances, it might be safer for us both if you too were not around to answer questions."

"I took the liberty of packing a small bag for myself."

In the limo to the airport, perhaps for the last time, Paul flicked through the Financial Review. There was a small article with a black and white photograph he recognised. Recently appointed to the board of their very own bank was Robertson Mooney who it said had been consulting to the bank and Interpol for the past few months on international currency movements.

Should he show the boss?

In other news, through a series of circumstances, marginally marred by some of her lesser friends suggesting conspicuous consumption played a part, Meg was invited to become an ambassador for the CIVC in Australia. (That's the Comite Interprofessionel du Vin de Champagne). During her first year in office consumption of champagne in this thirsty little nation rose from three million bottles to three and a half million. Despite her sparkling appearances during that period, it cannot all be attributed to her. Boring stuff like the appreciating Australian dollar played a part. Although in the headquarters of the Comite in Epernay, word of mouth ensured that many of its male members made a point of travelling Downunder for promotional trips just to meet her.

She and Robertson never linked up, although they remained good friends in spite of one evening in the Opera House Car park, many champagnes after a performance, when a misread suggestion to consummate their friendship resulted in some embarrassment, a torn garment and a tiny piece of brown glass in Robertson's knee.

Mum and Dad could not have been happier. Ellie and Tim were constant sources of amusement and amazement. Ted did not wake up one morning and was found perfectly asleep on his favourite paving. Dad lifted several bricks, dug a generous grave, and placed him underneath. Monty still roams the neighbourhood, a triumph of domestication. Taking all he needs and offering what is needed. The following summer he did not have a cicada to talk to so he slept alone where the wall was hot.

Merac and Sondrine learned the meaning of sleep.

It is where we go when we are comfortable with the world we are resting from. For months they trembled, sleepless themselves, as Pix drew perfectly comfortable breaths. She would have no trouble with sleep for the rest of her life.

Sondrine took her daughter on a series of little journeys. Some so very basic but necessary because she had missed them at earlier stages of her life. The nicer ones were pure discovery. For mother and daughter.

There was also: Hullo school. Study. Sport. Gatherings. Friends.

Merac sat on the lounge. He held his wife's hand.

Their daughter skipped across to them. So much
energy so late in the day. She held a book she had taken
from her father's shelves. There was so much crammed
into his study so there was nothing she could do to
make it more untidy. He was working every day, but
without the intensity of the previous summer.

"Daddy, tell me about cicadas."

He began to tell her the boring bits, the
background any student of biology could start with.

Pix soon began to doze resting against her mother
fingering her sleeve. The pattern and texture of her
sweater was more interesting to a sleepy seven year
old than Daddy's words.

Merac reached to the table beside him and took up
his notebook with the thick soft pencil.

He turned a page that was already covered with
drawings he had done of Gerry nudging up to him, so
excited on the night he returned from his Quest. Even
with the thick strokes of black on white you could tell
the jewels were glowing.

He started the fresh page with a headline.

He very rarely wrote headlines.

It said

'Gerry's Summer.'

Chapter Thirty

The workmen don't go to the top of the Opera House every day. When they do, there are a series of internal stairs and walkways they must climb. Utilitarian, made from rough sawn wood and steel pipe. Nothing as fine as the overarching shells, merely a means to take you higher. The swelling beauty of the tiled sails the world loves is accessed by quite ugly staircases. As you make your way up inside you can see glimpses way down to auditoriums and foyers and you are drawn closer to the building's essential structure, its internal skeleton beautifully cast in soft grey concrete. The surfaces are so smooth you'd associate them with a more delicate structure. There are few straight lines. Every curving spar repeats and repeats Utzon's homage to the sphere. They are massive, but a certain sensitivity informs the finish.

As you make it to another steel mesh platform the final climb awaits you. Not only is this part of your climb not very elegant, it is very scary. It is no time to discover you are claustrophobic or bothered by vertigo. A steel ladder starts vertically but gradually curves over on itself until you are crawling horizontally with your back just below the concrete spine of the largest sail. A door is opened above you and then you emerge into the blazing light of a Sydney day close to the peak of the sail. Behind you is a trough diving steeply down between the eye-filling world of white tiles. On each side they flow, tight and perfect, curving alarmingly away from you. Standing up the first time your knees will tremble as you adjust to a view very few have seen.

Some of you may have climbed the mossy slabs of Villa d'Este; the salty slipperiness of the Giant's Causeway; the pretty modesty of the Spanish Steps; the more challenging elevations fronting Sacre Coeur. You may even have survived the stone tortures of Huanya Picchu, or the pyramids in Ankor Wat or Teotihuacan.

You like interior climbs? You would have curved your body to fit inside the double skin of St Peters in Rome or the Duomo in Florence or bowed to the Grand Gallery up the middle of the Great Pyramid.

You may even have enjoyed the Bridgeclimb on the neighbouring Harbour Bridge, but the climb to the top of the main sail of Sydney's Opera House is a limited edition special. Nobody tells their friends about it because nobody much has done it.

On a summer evening, clear as a bell, two men in the employ of the Opera House scrambled out to do their work. Arthur and Ernie. They were both excellent craftsmen in their day. Makers of fine tools. Ernie decades ago has been apprenticed and trained to be the best gas welder in the country. With a soft blue flame could weld together thin sheets of lead like delicate embroidery, and with a roaring nozzle of fire he could ripple layers of molten bronze to hold a cast iron wheel together.

Arthur in his younger days could turn a small shaft for a watch on a lathe designed to hold large motor car parts. He could roll a cigarette in one hand as his other hand with infinite delicacy fed the cross-slide and the tool to caress the spinning metal.

Now close to retirement these champions of lost arts were simply maintenance men.

As they straightened up, and looked back they could see the bulk of the city. They had a reasonable glimpse of the Botanic Gardens; and a clear view of the two old red gums on the grass above the cliff. They knew that spot well because they would often go up there to have a sandwich or a pie for lunch. Nice to get outside, sit on the warm grass. A view like that in the middle of the city. Not bad. All for free.

Below them was the lively lagoon of Circular Quay. Chopped by the ferries and other boats bringing people from the richer Harbour suburbs of Sydney and taking out tourists for lunchtime cruises or to Manly and the Zoo. They had a grand view of the bridge. It looked like they could almost toss a ball to the people on the Bridgeclimb.

But today they were here to work so it was really just so much water and trees.

Unnoticed by tourists and unshown in most photos is the curving trench of steps which marks the spine of the big white sail.

Ernie and Arthur had done their checks on the suspected problem further down, someone thought they had spotted some broken tiles, and found nothing. They now made their way back up.

Together these two, lit with a golden light seemed to be taking to the sky, like the walk of the gods towards Valhalla. Near the peak they looked back towards the city. Almost at their height the twin trees caught the last of the westering sun. Red gums in red light. From them and other trees in the Gardens a strum started up. The cicadas had something to say. First one with a cranky rattle of the tympani. Throat clearing. Then a second, third, fourth, tenth and hundredth. Phasing then aligning to a pure note. A chorus of happiness.

With his back to that happy racket Arthur pulled himself up to the topmost steps and noticed a blemish on the tiles.

He went to brush it off when it turned and looked at him.

A cicada. Sitting at the very top of the Opera House. No-one has explained what the cicada was seeking at that altitude.

"He's still moving."

"Chuck it." said Ernie, panting a dozen steps behind him.

"No. I'll take him home to my kids. They've never seen a greengrocer. They'd like him."

"My cat would like him, too. Chuck him off,"

"Nah, I'll take him home. You remember that cicada shell I picked up near those trees the other day where we have lunch? I took that home to show the kids and they said thanks a lot Dad that's not much use, how about a real one. Now I can show them a real one."

Gerry was picked up and pushed into a pocket in the front of the overalls. Upside down, his legs waved slowly. His wings were uselessly cramped. At the bottom of the pocket his back was in a seam with grains of dirt in it.

Gerry recognised the dirt from the base of the Twin Reds. The actual soil of his own tunnels. He began to climb as cicadas always must. This time he struggled to rise, not through moist dirt and eucalyptus roots, but denim. With traces of his ancestral soil on his legs the climber scratched to the top of the pocket. He cleared the edge and worked towards the strap on Arthur's shoulder.

"Hullo, mate. You trying to get out? OK, just hang on a sec."

Ha. You don't have to tell a cicada to hang on. There was more chance of Arthur dropping off the sails than Gerry slipping from his overalls.

The cicada chorus rose in volume. Arthur could never have been aware of the glow in the jewels of the cicada on his shoulder.

He straightened and turned to Ernie.

"Grab this mate, it's yours."

Arthur held out the heavy steel screwdriver but it slipped from his fingers.

The screwdriver bounced and arched. The ping of a stupid tool on concrete was something they had both heard a thousand times. They knew the fall was inevitable. You can't fight gravity. The bastard would clatter down the concrete until it hit the very lowest point it could find. All they could hope was that it didn't kill anyone.

They looked at each other as the cicada chorus held its power.

The screwdriver spun and leapt and somersaulted like no other inanimate object they had ever seen.

Flicking sunlight it clattered and landed on the top of Ernie's toolbox. It rolled to one side as though it was looking over the edge, then rolled back again and sat there waiting as though it knew it belonged there.

"Bugger me. Did you see that?" said Ernie. "Bloody amazing."

"You couldn't do that in a million years." said Arthur, genuinely amazed, knowing that what he had just seen was just not possible. He saw his mate silhouetted against the west as the sun lowered its flame, surrendering its glow into the arms of the city buildings.

A humble man and reverent man, he looked across the space for a moment, and felt balanced between cicadas and humans, the space surprisingly less than he thought.

He heard the chorus taken up around the foreshore. A mighty shrilling sound. A sound everybody knew, a background to every summer since long before the First Fleet. A sound so well known that people rarely stopped to listen. But a sound so pure and strong and clear you'd reckon even a screwdriver on a tool box could pick it up.

He felt for the cicada on his shoulder but it was gone.

What he had was a song.

A perfect song.